NEW YEAR'S NUISANCE

A HOLIDAY COZY MYSTERY BOOK 4

TONYA KAPPES

D1525699

TONYA KAPPES
WEEKLY NEWSLETTER

Want a behind-the-scenes journey of me as a writer?
The ups and downs, new deals, book sales, giveaways and more? I share it all!

As a special thank you for joining, you'll get an exclusive copy of my cross-over short story, *A CHARMING BLEND.* Go to Tonyakappes.com and click on subscribe in the upper right corner to join.

New Year's Nuisance

"Just because no one is in here at the moment doesn't mean I'm going to talk to you," I told him when we walked past the cute miniature display of Jubilee Inn, which showed Mayor Paisley, the Boston terrier, sitting on the stoop and having her photo taken with tourists.

A true-to-life activity that looked to be Kristine's addition to this year as the judge.

"It's not what you think." Darren had tried to make it around me, but the walk was so narrow he might knock something down, like a giant.

"It's not?" I gasped. My eyes traveled to one of the new additions, a tall castle with a window at the top. I guessed it was the fairy tale "Rapunzel" because Hillary Stevens was propped up against the castle. Her hair was knotted around it, and what appeared to be blood was coming out of her side.

CHAPTER ONE

"**D**on't even get me started on your replacement." Mae West wore a pair of black skintight leggings with a lime-green wool sweater and her fancy New York booties. I'd noticed those right off when she rolled into my hometown of Normal, Kentucky, a few years ago before I'd moved to Holiday Junction.

I mean literally rolled into town in a camper van.

She'd not stopped talking since walking off the airplane at the Holiday Junction airport, which was about the size of her camper van.

"Mae, this is Rhett Strickland." I barely got the words out between her breaths before a huge smile curled up on her face.

She abruptly stopped, flung a strand of her curly honey-blond hair behind her shoulder, and threw her arms around him.

"Rhett!" From her voice, she clearly thought he was someone he wasn't. "Nice to meet you. Any friend of Violet's is a friend of mine."

"Welcome to Holiday Junction." He peeled himself off Mae. His brows rose, and he looked at me with a half-cocked smile. "Are all the people from Kentucky this friendly? Because Violet sure wasn't this friendly the day I met her right in this very spot."

He grabbed the handle of Mae's luggage and jerked it to full extension so he could roll it behind him.

"I guess Violet'll have to bring you home for a visit." Mae wiggled her brows.

"Oh no." I cackled out loud and pinched off a piece of the bagel I'd gotten from the airport's small café while I'd waited for Mae's plane to land. "We aren't an item. Heck no."

A weird nervous laugh I'd not recognized came out of me.

"You said Strickland." Mae started to say something that didn't need to be said before I grabbed her by the elbow, jerking her to me.

"I'm so glad you called after the Christmas you had." I had to change the subject of my love life when I didn't even know what my love life was all about. "Let's get you in the car."

Rhett was a catch. Don't get me wrong. And we'd had a little spark between us. I'm talking tiny. Just a flicker, really. After there'd been too much going on in my new life to even think about lighting that wick, it was quickly put out.

On the other hand, his cousin, Darren, didn't seem like my type, and even though I wasn't on the prowl, he seemed to be around…. everywhere.

Over Halloween, we'd shared a kiss, but it'd never gone any further than that. By the way he'd slid me into his arms that night, I thought for sure I'd have a date to the New Year's Eve celebration, the famous Sparkle Ball, but he was like a cricket.

Silent during the day but loud at night.

Calling him "loud" was giving him too much credit. It was the bar he owned that was loud at night. The jiggle joint.

At least that was what I called it, even though the name on the solid door read BAR.

I didn't think I had to say much more than that it was… a jiggle joint. Truly, there was a lot more drinking, throwing darts, and rowdy chatter than jiggling going on.

I had to walk past the bar every night on my way home from my office at the *Junction Journal*, the local newspaper of which I was the editor in chief, photographer, journalist, and, well, all the things.

"Rhett is the security guard here at the airport," I told her.

We followed Rhett into the one-room terminal before he stopped shy of the one TSA agent and Dave.

Mae's eyes grew big when she saw Dave.

"Okay. You have no business talking about the strange animals we have back home." Mae laughed.

I bet she couldn't wait to tell people back home about him.

"He was the local rooster who was part of the security team. Dave was better than any sniffing security dog out there." Rhett was confident in telling Mae about Dave and a few of his rooster-sniffing stories. "And we have a dog for mayor."

"That I do know." Mae pointed at the jar on the podium where Dave and the TSA agent were perched. "What's that?"

"Those are worms—treats." Rhett picked up the jar. Dave clucked to life and stood tall like a soldier.

"I've seen it all." Mae turned to me and wagged a finger. "Don't you ever make fun of Normal again."

I smiled. Being around Mae brought a sense of familiarity that made me long for the comforts of home. Though I couldn't get back to Kentucky anytime soon, I was going to soak up all the joy it brought my soul to see her and gab about all the friends we knew.

Rhett unscrewed the lid off the jar and held it out for Mae, who took a dehydrated piece of worm.

"Just give it to him," Rhett instructed her and pretended to hold a piece for reference.

"Thanks, Dave." Mae threw her head back and laughed with her mouth wide open. "We might be hillbillies in Kentucky, but this town is strange," she whispered between us.

"When I saw Violet come in this morning to greet you, I was thinking she was sneaking off to some big interview. You know, I met her the day her plane made the emergency landing." Rhett continued to walk us through the one-room airport toward the door. "She certainly didn't like my uncle then and can barely be in the same room with him now."

"You're the police chief's nephew. Not son." Mae snapped her finger, and the emerald ring she wore flickered as the light inside the airport caught it.

"Mae," I gasped and grabbed her hand to look at the engagement ring Hank Sharp had given her. "I love it."

I did love it but was a little shocked it was an emerald.

"I keep forgetting you've been gone since I got engaged." She curled her hand in and pulled it to her chest as though she didn't want me to see it or talk about it. "Speaking of rings, you aren't going to believe what I'm about to tell you."

"I can't wait." I was giggly with excitement to have Mae here, even if it was only for a few days and most of those would be taken up by writing the coverage of the New Year festivities for the *Junction Journal*.

Holiday Junction was a small town, just like my hometown. And true to its name, they celebrated every single holiday. But the big ones—you know, Easter, Thanksgiving, Fourth of July, Christmas—now those celebrations were over-the-top.

The Sparkle Ball was this year's theme for the New Year's Eve celebration.

When Mae called to wish me a merry Christmas, I had mentioned the big Sparkle Ball and how the *Junction Journal* was sponsoring it. Within seconds, she invited herself, and here she was, a couple of days away from the turn of the new year.

Trust me when I say I was surprised. It wasn't like Mae and I were best friends in Normal. Honestly, quite the opposite. We'd fought tooth and nail, butted heads, to be truthful. Never in a million years did I ever think I'd be celebrating the turn of a new year with Mae West.

"This is far as I go, ladies." Rhett stopped shy of the double sliding doors leading to the outside world. "Duty calls. The next plane should be arriving, um"—Rhett joked and checked his phone—"two days from now."

Holiday Junction had very few flights in and out, but there was a much bigger airport an hour or so away. If anyone needed a flight, they could drive there.

"It was nice to meet you, Rhett." Mae had really put on the

Southern charm, a far cry from when I'd met her years ago, when she showed a hard exterior. "I sure hope to see you at the fancy Sparkle Ball."

"You sure will." Rhett said his goodbyes.

It was nice to see this side of her, and it made me happy she was here. We'd never had any sort of sleepover or true get-together just as friends. More times than not, we met during my interviewing days as a reporter for Channel Two news, my daily talk show, or for the *Normal Gazette*.

"I have to admit I was a little nervous when you told me you were coming out," I said and walked out of the airport. "Are you okay?" I asked, pointing at the trolley stop sign.

"Yeah. You know." Mae wiggled her finger in the air. "Wedding stuff plus Mary Elizabeth and, well, the whole Sharp family saga."

She left the word hanging and looked out into the distance.

"That's gorgeous." She pointed at the snow-covered landscape where the mountains rose in the distance. A few of the peaks were hidden behind a veil of white, as if reaching up to touch the sky.

"And this crisp air." She sucked in a deep breath.

"It is amazing here." I took in the trees, which were coated in a layer of frost. The branches were heavy with snow, and the ground was a blanket of white. The snow crunched underfoot as we walked into the glass enclosure to wait for the next ride into town.

"It really is pretty here." She looked at me, and her eyes dipped.

There was more to Mae's visit than just a visit, but I'd give her space, and in her own time, she'd tell me. I had to ask about the word she'd let dangle before she'd noticed the landscape.

"Saga?" I asked and saw Goldie Bennett was at the helm of the trolley. The shimmery red-sequined shirt looked like Goldie was starting her own personal New Year's party.

Ding, ding. The clanking trolley bell clapped as it approached. Goldie slammed the brakes on and pushed the lever that swung the door open.

"Welcome to Holiday Junction, Mae!" Goldie blew on the dazzling, shiny gold-and-silver fringe blowout on one of those cone-shaped cardboard New Year's Eve hats with fuzz all over the edges. "We are so excited you're here. Climb on in."

"Okay." Mae's eyes lit up. When she took a step up, she glanced back at me. "And I thought this was going to be a boring week."

"Nope. Normal, Kentucky, has nothing on Holiday Junction." My body shivered as the goose bumps crawled along my skin.

CHAPTER TWO

"We've been hearing all about you and Violet." Goldie slammed the handle to close the doors before she threw the trolley in gear. "I saved this bench for you two."

Mae and I sat down. Goldie looked in the large rearview mirror to make sure we were properly seated before she punched the gas pedal.

The trolley was open-air during the warmer months with zip-down plastic-style windows for chilly weather.

"She did." Mae leaned back and looked at me.

"Yeppers. We heard you two weren't the closest of friends." Goldie talked way too much, and apparently, I had too.

"Is that right?" Mae smiled. I could see her little brains twisting inside that head of hers.

"But it seems all that fussing and fighting is all over now. No need to bring up the past." Goldie swung the trolley out of the parking lot of the airport, one eye on the road and one eye fixed on us from the rearview mirror.

"Sounds to me like someone is bringing up the past." Mae shoved a big patch of her curly hair behind her shoulder.

"How's the wedding plans?" Goldie continued to spill her guts about all the things I'd told her about Mae.

"You know about that too?" Mae questioned, letting out a heavy sigh. Her tone of voice made me squirm a little, causing me to look out the trolley window. "I guess you have made this place home." She nudged me.

"You know, I was stranded here a few days before I decided to take the job at the *Junction Journal*." I gulped and pulled my knit cap down on my forehead a little more. My long blond hair was braided into two ponytails. "Goldie is about the only mode of transportation I take these days."

"You mean in the daylight?" Goldie threw me off. "During the nights she likes to hop on Darren's scooter. At least that's what I've heard."

"Darren." Mae smacked the palm of her hand on her head. "That the police chief's son?"

"Yeah," I said with a flat tone and held on for dear life as Goldie took the sharp turn toward town. "And I just want you to know that I'm no way on Darren's moped at night."

"He drives a moped?" Mae's brow shot up with an amused look on her face. "How old is he?"

"Stop it. This town is so small you don't need a car. Please, the trolley is perfect to get around." I shook my head. "We can talk later about Darren."

It was my way of telling her, though I was sure she already could tell, that we couldn't talk in front of Goldie.

Goldie got it too.

"Did Violet tell you anything about our little town?" Goldie didn't even wait to hear Mae's answer because she went into full-on tourist mode, just like she did when she picked up tourists at the airport.

"We are a small seaside, mountainside, and countryside town." Goldie pointed out along the route in each direction. "You can pick your poison and stay in the heart of any of these places. I do not believe Violet has yet experienced all we have to offer."

"I did notice the mountains right off." Mae looked out into the woodsy area we were passing by. "It seems like you've got all the terrains covered here in Holiday Junction."

8

"We do. Like I said, pick your poison. But with the snow these days, I'd say hiking is out of the question. From what I hear, your hometown is pretty much all woods, mountains, and trails." Goldie nodded.

"My goodness. It sounds like you've been to Kentucky," Mae noted.

"Only through the eyes of Millie Kay." Goldie brought the trolley to an abrupt stop to let off other passengers.

"I've only explored downtown," I confirmed. "Goldie also gives trolley tours around town for donations. All donations go to the Holiday Committee. And Mama is on the Holiday Committee."

"Honey, she isn't on it. Millie Kay just got elected as president." Goldie took the quick turn on the main road leading to the Jubilee Inn.

"That's fun." Mae's voice rose. "I guess it means they—your parents —are going to stay here?"

"Mm-hmm." My lips tucked together, and I slowly nodded.

"From what I understand, you like to hike, and we have some of the best trails in the mountains but only during the warmer months. I expect you back here to take advantage of them." Goldie was good at her job at talking up the town. "We had a bit of a slow economy until the village council. We were a village, not a town. Until the Village Council decided to do what our name said and promote every single holiday. That was when the tourism picked up and, like you Southern people like to say, it was all she wrote."

Goldie glanced back.

"I've been studying up on my Southern phrases, and Millie Kay has been a big help." Goldie went on to tell Mae about the houses along the route once we made it into the village. "Notice the row of houses on each side of the street? These are original to the town and very big with lots of yard space. These houses stay in the family for years. Like the Stricklands."

Goldie pointed out the Strickland compound when we passed it. If the size of the house alone didn't scream wealth and power, the tall wrought-iron-and-brick fencing around the compound did.

The lights dotted along the sidewalk had beach-ball-sized mirrored balls dangling from the dowel rods, all dressed up for the Sparkle Ball.

The large trees that normally gave shade to the many people during the hot months were barren. But they still looked pretty with the leftover white twinkle lights the committee had kept up for the New Year celebration. The lights were meant to be easy to use for Christmas one week and the New Year's festival the next.

"How are your parents?" Mae asked, bringing us back to the topic. Then she added, "We sure did miss Millie Kay's outside decorations at their home."

"Don't worry." I rolled my eyes. "You're going to get to see all that here. When she heard you were coming, she decided to keep up the Christmas tree in one room and the other rooms decorated for New Year's. It was like Holiday Junction was established just for Mama's kind."

Mama was Holiday Junction before I'd even heard of Holiday Junction. I grew up with the house decorated for not only the upcoming holiday but also the season. Mama changed out the bedding, the wreaths, the little whatnots sitting around the house, and even the dishes we ate on.

"So, what's with this Darren thingy?" Mae asked me, making me shift uncomfortably in my seat.

"We have plenty of time to talk about that. I want to hear your big plans." I knew if I could get Mae talking about snagging Hank Sharp, the most wanted bachelor in Normal, then it'd take the heat off me.

"None." She shrugged, setting off my radar that something wasn't quite right with Mae West and Hank Sharp.

By the way she reacted, I knew something was up because their wedding was supposed to be a big to-do. Everyone in Normal was talking about it long before Hank had proposed.

"Next stop!" Goldie sucked in a deep breath. "Jubilee Inn!"

She brought the trolley to a complete stop and shoved the lever that opened the door. Cold air swept in around my ankles. I knew I should've worn longer socks today. There was an unseasonable cold front coming from the mountains on the back side of town, and from what I understood, it was going to hang around for a while.

"Isn't that cute." Mae referred to the small inn.

The Jubilee Inn was adorned with sparkling lights and festive decorations. A large banner read Happy New Year! and streamers in various shades of silver and gold hung from the roof.

A balloon arch in the shape of the numbers of the upcoming year stood at the entrance, greeting guests with a burst of color.

A red carpet led to the doors, where a pair of doormen stood in formal attire, ready to welcome visitors.

A crowd of people had gathered around a small stage at the foot of the steps of the entrance, waiting for the town celebrity to come out so they could get their photo with her.

Mayor Paisley, the French bulldog.

"This is your stop." I pointed out the window at the Jubilee Inn.

"What?" Mae jerked around, and her purse fell down. All the contents scattered across the trolley floor.

"I have to go to work for a little bit, so I thought I'd let you get settled into the inn." I bent down to help her pick up the items. "I'll text you a time for supper so you can see my parents."

"Wait." She froze when I handed her the lipstick tube. "You mean I'm not staying with you?"

"Um." After she'd told me she was coming, I'd never responded with where she was going to stay. I had things to do.

Important things to do.

Secret things to do.

Merry Maker things to do.

Plus, I had to beg, steal, cheat, and borrow for the room we did get for Mae because Kristine Whitlock, the owner, said they were all filled up.

But as a reporter, I knew every single hotel in the United States always kept *one* room vacant just in case someone important came to town.

This week, the important person was Mae West.

Really, I didn't have to do all of those things to get the room. I just had to run a few free ads in the journal for the Jubilee Inn. They didn't need the ads, but I guess Kristine wanted something to barter for, and the cute photo of Mayor Paisley in her New Year's Eve hat and gold bowtie always got a lot of clicks for the online feature of the week, which listed all the festival activities for each day.

"I thought you'd want your own place." I was so happy her ink pen had rolled underneath the bench so I didn't have to look at her while I reached far back to retrieve it. As I did, I tried hard to not look at all the gum stuck up underneath the wood slats of the bench.

"No. I want to stay with you." Mae's eyes dipped as the disappointment settled on them. "I never mentioned a hotel, inn, or motel." She cleared her throat. "Goldie, we need to go to Violet's work, please."

"M'kay." Goldie leaned way over, grabbed the lever handle, and tugged the doors closed.

"Not yet," I said to stop her.

"M'kay." Goldie shoved the lever back, leaning over again. "Hurry up. I've got other stops." Her hand never left the lever.

"Violet's office." Mae used a more demanding tone.

Goldie closed the door.

"No. Mae is getting off here." The frustration came out of my voice like all the confetti released from a balloon popped on New Year's Eve.

Goldie opened the door.

"Then just take me back to the airport. I'm going home." Mae planted herself back on the bench, with her purse tucked up to her chest.

"Which is it?" Goldie asked out of exhaustion. "The *Junction Journal* or the Holiday Junction Airport?"

"The *Junction Journal*," I muttered as I started to come up with excuses to leave my tiny little over-the-garage apartment in the middle of the night to fulfil my job as the town's newest Merry Maker.

The biggest secret anyone in town could keep.

CHAPTER THREE

"This is amazing." Mae stood in front of the seaside cottage with all her pieces of luggage rolled next to her. "I stepped off the airplane and felt like I was in the Swiss Alps. I ride a trolley and feel like I'm back at home in the woods. I step off the trolley and I'm at the beach. Only it's winter at the beach."

The snow danced in the air that came off the ocean and fell gently from the clear, bright-blue sky onto the sand, forming a beautiful and peaceful scene.

The ocean was a deep, dark blue, and the whitecaps of the waves seemed to shimmer in the sunlight. The air was crisp and cold, and the smell of the sea was strong and salty. As the snow continued to fall, it blanketed the ground in a soft, white layer, creating a picturesque winter wonderland.

The entire scene was serene and calming, and it was a perfect start to Mae's visit.

"This is an amazing place for an office." The surprised expression on Mae's face told me she'd not really pictured the village when I described it to her over the phone. "It's truly a beautiful little town."

"Village. Holiday Junction is a village," I corrected her. "But the office is a different story. I got the owners of the newspaper to renovate and move the *Junction Journal* office here. It used to be in a house on their compound."

Yes. Compound as in the Strickland compound. Louise and Marge Strickland, sisters-in-law, owned the *Junction Journal*. When I literally landed into the Village, the sisters-in-law were in the process of shutting down the local newspaper.

It was my idea after we'd reached an agreement for me to take a job, running everything. They accepted my request to move the office from their home to the cottage Rhett owned. It just so happened to be seaside. A bonus if anyone were to ask me.

Regardless of how we got here and bypassing the details, the office had been successfully renovated. Even Mama worked for the *Junction Journal* now, though "worked" was a word that was used very loosely when it came to Millie Kay Rhinehammer.

"I honestly love being here," I told Mae as we both stood on the small porch of the cottage and overlooked the scenery that lay out in front of us. "I have all the views." I pointed behind me at the mountain range. "And I even have a little bit of forest, though here I'd call it more woods than forest."

Mae sucked in a deep breath. I could feel something was going on with her, but I wasn't going to press it. As a matter of fact, I'd figured I'd see some big celebrity in town over Mae West any day. For her to be standing here with me, when I had no doubt she clapped when I decided to leave Normal. That was how close we really were.

Or maybe it was when I called her for advice the same day the emergency landing took place that we actually had something in common.

Nosy.

"You sure do seem to have settled in." Mae's smile didn't reach the corners of her eyes. "And I can't wait to hear all about Darren," she said as soon as I opened the door of the office.

"Come on in." I held the door for her. "I have no idea who is here or not here because no one really has a car. Mama has a golf cart."

Mae laughed, which warmed my heart.

"Violet, I hope you got your friend settled in at the Inn because you've still got to write all the copy for the New Year's Day events outside of the Sparkle Ball. They made so many changes to help promote the mini-village contest," Louise Strickland, one of the owners of the *Junction Journal*, hollered out from the back of the small seaside cottage. "Don't forget Darren's band is playing us into the new year, so you have to print that too."

"Darren has a band?" Mae was giddy.

"The Mad Fiddlers." I tried not to laugh at the ridiculous name. "He's a fiddle player."

"Oh dear me," Mae said, her Southern accent falling from her lips. She put her hand up to her heart.

The sound of bracelets jingling from the hallway signaled that Louise was coming to greet us.

"Oh. Hello." Louise, Darren's mama, had on a long-sleeved, floor-sweeping gold cardigan with a gold headscarf to match.

She was the more eccentric of the two Strickland women and very friendly.

"Louise, this is my friend Mae." As I introduced them, Louise stuck her hand out, but Mae went straight for the hug.

"You people must all do that." Louise stiffened and gave Mae a tidy pat on the back.

"Rhett said the same thing, and I told him we hug around our partner as a greeting. Just because I'm not in Normal doesn't mean my manners go flying out the door." Mae pulled back. "I love your town, er, village. Violet didn't tell me it was this cute. Nor did she tell me Darren was in a band."

"I hope you found your room at the inn acceptable. It took a lot of free ads to acquire that room." Louise was never one to beat around the bush.

"Violet." Mae gasped and blinked her big, long lashes. "You didn't tell me that."

"It's fine. Mae is going to stay with me in my garage." I waved it off, not looking at Louise. "What were you saying about the Sparkle Ball?" I changed the subject. "The mini-village?"

"Nothing. I can do it." Louise smiled and looked between Mae and me.

"No. No." Mae shook her head. "I insisted I come to see where Violet worked, and now that I have, I think I'll go take a walk around town."

"Did I hear someone I know?" Mama appeared around the threshold of her office just to the left of the front door.

"Millie Kay!" Mae squealed. Excitement filled the air as both women grabbed on to one another like the clock on New Year's just struck midnight.

"Look at you. Pretty as a picture." Mama held Mae at an arm's length. "Let me get a look at you."

"You are always so kind, and I can't help but say you do wonders for my ego." Mae twinkled like the glass on a mirror ball when the disco lights hit it. "Listen, we will have a lot of time to chat later. Violet needs to get her work done."

"Then I'll take you around the Village. It ain't fittin' for you to go around by yourself. Besides, I need to drop off my miniature pies at the Welcome Center to be judged for the mini-village. I'll be right back." Mama hurried back into her office.

"That settles it, then." Louise rubbed her hands together.

"Are you sure?" I asked Mae, knowing I not only had stuff to do in the *Journal*'s online section but also needed to slip away to do some of the Merry Maker activities.

"I'm positive." Mae offered up a nice, warm Southern smile. "I've not been walking in the sand in years. It'll be nice to put my toes in it. And I'm excited to spend some time with Millie Kay. It was always such a joy to have her when she sat in on the National Park Committee meetings."

"Honey," Louise said, shivering, "the water is freezing. You don't want to put your toes in it."

Mama walked out of the office with her coat zipped up to her chin, a hat on her head, and her pocketbook tucked in the crook of her elbow.

"I'll be fine." Mae gave me one last hug before she and Mama started to walk out the front door. "Keep me posted about later today."

"I'll text you. Thank you, Mama!" I shut the door behind them and

16

for a moment watched Mae skip down the sidewalk. She disappeared in the dunes between the cottage where Mama parked her golf cart.

"Your friend is lovely." Louise had waited there with me. "But I get a sense you're happy she's gone out with your mama."

"I do have a lot to do, and when I had Goldie drop her off at the inn, Mae thought she was staying with me." I would have to explain because it did take a lot for me to get the Strickland women to agree to the free ads in exchange for giving me Mae's room.

"Don't worry. I'm sure we can get someone to stay in that room, even if they are only there after the Sparkle Ball because they've had too much fun and can't get home." Louise laughed. "I put the itinerary on your desk. I think they need to get on the website as soon as possible."

"No problem. I'll do that right now." I unzipped my coat, took it off, and hung it on the coatrack next to the door.

I expected Louise to go back to the kitchen and do whatever it was she was doing there, since neither she nor Marge had anything to do with the *Junction Journal*. I had full control and liked it that way, though Mama did work here and did some of the research.

Mama was darn good at finding out all the things about people. She was relentless. She'd dig on every social media site and get background checks to find all the details on someone we were either featuring in an article or just plain nosy about.

I followed Louise into my office, which was across the hall from Mama's.

"We need to get the new details for the ribbon-cutting ceremony they are going to hold for the mini-village. It's something last-minute." Louise slapped a sticky note on the computer on my desk.

"The mini-village," I groaned.

This town was so weird. They had this mini-village they added to every year. It was a large-scale model of the Village featured at the Welcome Center.

It was a competition. Mama had never ever done a mini anything in her life. So when she heard about this competition, Mama couldn't just let it go. She had to dive all in, especially since the prize was free weekly groceries for a year.

The quicker I got the information up on the online paper, the faster Louise would get out of my hair so I could attend to more important things.

Namely, working as the Merry Maker.

The Village Merry Maker was something I'd never wanted to be. It came with duties I never wanted to take part in and was shoved on me by a past Merry Maker.

I loved the idea and the things the Merry Maker stood for but holding all the responsibility on my shoulders and not telling anyone I was *the* Merry Maker was a whole other level of stress I didn't need.

"Mama has been working on her miniature for a few months now," I told Louise, who stood over my shoulder while I typed in exactly what she wanted me to put in the article.

"Explain to me one more time about this tradition?" I asked so that when I went to the Welcome Center to take the photos for the paper, I'd at least have some more in-depth knowledge in case I needed to ask questions.

Journalists loved to have all the facts.

"It started way before I was born, but as it's been told to me and passed down generation to generation"—Louise stood over me—"it was a hobby for some of the women back then, and it turned into them getting together to make a replica of our town with the minis."

"The research I did said how it caught on and how they added to it every year." I told her that so many people were doing minis and trying to contribute to the replica, that it got so big there was no more room at the library, so it was moved to the Welcome Center, and that that was when they decided to make it a contest that added the winners' minis to the collection.

"That's why it's very important to get this in the paper as soon as possible." It was Louise's way of telling me to stop talking and start typing. "There's even themes. And this year's theme is nursery rhymes."

"Why nursery rhymes?" I asked.

"This year, Holiday Junction's population increased because of the number of babies born here. The most in the last decade," Louise said.

"That's more of a story to me." I thought about how that would make a good piece in the special New Year's Day edition of the paper.

"The mini-village is really something to see." Louise offered, "Why don't I walk with you to the Welcome Center after you get the rest of the online paper up?"

Louise didn't really mean that as a question, and I was fine with it. Mae was being entertained by Mama. From the window, I'd watched them take off toward the beach, where Mae had jumped out of the enclosed golf cart with no shoes on.

I smiled.

If you'd told me Mae West and I would be good friends even a year ago, I'd have called you crazy.

CHAPTER FOUR

I'd suggested to Louise that we walk to the Welcome Center instead of taking the trolley even though the snow was really coming down. She'd met me with a little pushback, but when I pointed out that Mama and Mae were still galivanting along the shoreline, Louise had agreed it would be nice to visit.

Really, it was just cold weather, and deep down, I wanted to walk by the lighthouse on our way up to Holiday Park just in case Darren was leaving. It was about the time of the morning when he went to check on the jiggle joint.

I needed him to meet Mae and realize I wouldn't be able to get all the Merry Maker jobs done without some help. He had landed himself a co-Merry Maker position when he snooped around and found out I was the Merry Maker. He pointed out very clearly that I wasn't the most discreet at it.

"This is such a cute town. Um, village." Mae was walking ahead with Mama. Mama was pointing out all the little shops and which ones Mae had to go to while she was here.

"You'll have plenty of time to go while Violet works," Louise told Mae. "But I insist you come for supper."

"Where are you going?" I asked Louise when she stopped in front of the pottery shop where everyone went, including Mama, to make their minis. The display in the window was darling.

In fact, it reminded me of what the Sparkle Ball would look like. I'd never been, but everyone in town talked about how gorgeous the ballroom was to see. This year's theme was glitter and glitz.

"I've got to pop in to get a mini that Matthew and I had made for the addition to the police department." Louise hadn't even mentioned they'd made something.

"Addition?" I asked, wondering just how they would fit into the judging.

"Don't worry. It's part of the tradition." Louise plucked the gloves off her fingers one by one. As she put the gloves in her pocket, a girl walked out of the shop and nearly bowled Louise over. "Excuse me!" Louise hollered out to the girl, but she used her hands to throw the hoodie of her jacket up around her head.

"She's so rude," Louise said. "I think that's the person who ran into me earlier this morning when I was coming from Brewing Beans."

"Who was that?" Mama asked. "Maybe I should teach a manners class."

Mama had been trying to find her niche ever since she moved to Holiday Junction. At one point, she wanted to be a baker or even teach classes at the Incubator, a room in the back of the Freedom Diner where people could come and bake or cook to hone their skills.

Then she wanted to be in charge of various groups and committees. Then Daddy moved here, and well, trying to do things with him took up a lot of Mama's time because in some weird universe in her head, she'd been dead set on divorcing him.

For the time being, she appeared to be satisfied with Daddy, and they were still married, both living here in Holiday Junction.

Now she seemed to be fixated on this miniature adventure. As long as she was happy and stayed out of my personal life, I was more than happy to let her find her own bliss.

It only took one instant for Mama to come up with an idea. That one instant was just now, when the girl ran into Louise and didn't say sorry, my bad, excuse me—nothing.

"That's Hillary Stevens. Poor thing." Louise tsked. "She's always been the town nuisance. Her family says she can't help it."

"You mean something ain't firing right?" Mama asked and tapped her temple.

"No. She's a smart girl, but she just has a hard time being nice." Louise's observation of the girl made my heart hurt. "When she doesn't like something, she'll destroy it in a minute. Take Ceramic Celebration." Louise gestured to the pottery shop. "Denise Kenner told me how radical Hillary had gotten about change. The girl doesn't like change at all. In fact..." Louise looked around as if she were searching for the right words. "Matthew had to pay Hillary a visit after one of the town council meetings where they changed some law because she'd decided to protest by throwing rotten tomatoes at the courthouse and the library."

"Library?" Mama asked as though vandalizing the courthouse wasn't odd too.

"They hold the meetings there for the village's small businesses. Kinda like what a chamber of commerce would do in larger towns." Louise shrugged and went to tug on the shop door. "Looks like she's mad again." Louise shook her head and headed inside.

"Manners class?" I heard Mae encourage Mama where there didn't need to be any encouragement.

The two of them strolled around and talked about the shop, Mama telling her that she'd take her to the Bubbly Boutique for some cute earrings as she showed hers to Mae. They also made a date to go to Brewing Beans for a cup of hot coffee.

"Don't forget Emily's Treasures." I wanted to make sure Mama kept Mae busy so I could get in some free time to do at least the main job of the Merry Maker.

Find a place to host the New Year's celebration.

Yes. The Sparkle Ball was technically the big shebang with the glittery ball, flashing lights, renewed spirit, "Auld Lang Syne," and all that, but the Merry Maker's job was to find a location in Holiday Junction where everyone could come to do a final toast and send-off to the holiday. That was a job I could do, but it also came along with a life-size, painted cutout that depicted the holiday.

In this case, I'd asked Vern McKenna, a past Merry Maker and local carpenter, to make them for me. Little did I realize I had to be the one hauling those things all over town without anyone seeing me. Doing that proved to be more difficult than I'd initially thought.

That was where Darren came in. He snuck around at all hours of the night and had caught me struggling with the sign of a different Merry Maker job. I told him he had to help now that he knew my secret identity.

And his muscles were appealing, too, though I'd never say it out loud.

"Then we better hurry if you're going to be taking Mae all over the place," I said and picked up the pace, knowing we were about to pass the jiggle joint. I didn't want to linger past there because I didn't want to look like I was seeking out Darren.

I called the dive bar the jiggle joint because more than loose change jiggled its way down the jukebox, if you know what I mean. Not a place for a lady. Unless you were Mama. She loved going in there for what she called a toddy for the body.

There were no windows to the outside world, just the black metal door that took you into the bar, so there was no way I could see inside. Still, the off chance of running into Darren was not likely, but I'd at least like to get some eyes on him so he'd see I needed his help.

While the thoughts of how I would pull off the duties of the Merry Maker while Mae was here swirled in my head, Mama and Mae continued to talk about our hometown and gossip about what everyone back home was doing.

"And Ty Randal got married." Mae knocked the wind out of me.

"Ty?" I asked, since I'd not even known he was dating. Last I knew, he was running his family diner and helping his father raise his siblings, since his mother had passed. "To who?"

"Ellis Sharp." Mae's tone told me this was what she'd been wanting to tell me.

"Ellis?" My jaw literally dropped. "As in Hank's sister? Your soon-to-be sister-in-law?"

"Mm-hmm." By the way Mae slowly nodded and glanced over her shoulder at me, I could tell Ellis was pulling an Ellis. "That was my big news."

She'd pulled so many Ellises as a teenager. Hank always got the short end of the deal.

"I'm sorry. She can't stand not being in the limelight." I hated to point it out, but Mae knew it.

"Yep. That's kinda what happened. We were hosting a dinner to announce our wedding day, and let's just say when Ellis showed up with the big announcement"—Mae sighed, the condensation of her breath hitting the cold air that puffed out of her mouth—"it took the joy out of telling them the date, but it also took the heat off of me. It was a bit of a catch-22."

"Honey, Ellis Sharp has always been so tacky. She chewed gum in the church loft." Millie Kay nodded. "There's nothing tackier than being tacky." She lifted her chin in the air and led the way to the lighthouse. "Manners. People lack manners."

Mama wasn't going to get her idea of teaching a manners class out of her head.

The lighthouse stood tall and proud against the elements of winter, its beacon shining brightly through the snowy mist and over the frozen waves of the ocean.

The lighthouse looked like a beautiful, peaceful place to visit on a snowy beach day. My eyes slid up to the top where the small black metal fence reminded me of the first time Darren had kissed me. I licked my lips, recalling just how his soft lips felt against mine.

"You know"—Mama pointed at the lighthouse, bringing me out of my memory—"Violet's boyfriend lives there."

"Darren?" Mae trilled.

"He's not my boyfriend, Mama." I wished she'd stop referring to him as that.

"Then why do you sneak out at night?" Mama shrugged and continued to walk, not looking at me. "Every time the gate on the side of the house squeaks and your daddy and I look out, Darren is sneaking in."

"He's not sneaking." Oh no. I honestly had no idea they saw him coming to meet with me as we made our plans as co-Merry Makers.

Mae laughed.

"Millie Kay, I reckon she'll tell us when she's ready." Mae lifted her shoulders with a shrug and curled her hand inside of Mama's elbow.

I might've meandered a little behind them, hoping Darren would see us walking along the sidewalk since you could see everything out of the lighthouse windows. I should know. I'd been there a few times, and I loved standing up at the top.

We had plans to meet tonight so we could walk to see Vern, but that wasn't going to happen if Mae stayed with me, which looked like it would be the case.

"This is really cute." I could hear Mae talking to Mama about the sidewalk leading up through the small wooded area between Holiday Park and the seaside.

Mama was giving Mae the rundown and had picked up the speed. Thank goodness because it was getting a lot chillier with the gray clouds moving along the sky, hiding what little sun was out.

Mama had told Mae all about the Leading Ladies and pointed out the amphitheater as well as the lake where all the paddleboats had been covered for the winter. She told Mae about the fountain and all the fun activities the town did during the different holidays as though she'd lived here all her life.

"But I have to take you to the Bubbly Boutique." Mama stopped shy of us walking straight toward the Welcome Center, where the library, hospital, government buildings, and police department were located. "Do you mind taking these on down to the village while I take Mae to shop?"

Mama asked me but shoved the bubble-wrapped pieces in my coat pocket.

"Real quick?" I asked, hoping that meant a few hours so I could somehow get in touch with Darren to tell him about our change of plans.

"We might stop by Brewing Beans to warm up first." Mama rubbed her gloved hands together. "It's cold. We can't try on clothes if it's too cold."

"Yes. I'll be fine." I looked at Mae. "Do you want to go?"

"Of course she does. Mae lived in New York City and loves good quality clothing." Mama's eyes drew up and down me, like I didn't like good clothes.

I did. In fact, before Mae moved to my hometown, I was the best-dressed woman in town. I had to be because I was a news reporter and hosted my own morning show. I did miss that, but I did not miss getting all dolled up and worrying if I'd gotten enough sleep to the point that I had to pile on the makeup to cover up my dark circles.

Mama didn't let Mae even confirm she wanted to go. Mama grabbed Mae and dragged her past me, turning right down the main street of Holiday Junction, where they'd explore all the cute boutiques.

If I'd not had to take Mama's miniature pies to her display, I'd have turned around, marched right back to the lighthouse, and knocked on Darren's door so we could finalize this task for the New Year's holiday.

He'd been dragging his feet, and I wasn't sure why. I almost felt like he was avoiding me.

"You know what?" I told myself and twirled around on the toes of my shoes. "Mama's minis can wait."

There was no doubt in my mind Mama was going to keep Mae busy by showing her off to everyone in town. Mama had been waiting for someone from Normal to come visit. She was proud of our hometown, which made me question why she stayed here after she and Daddy had settled their differences.

The clouds had completely covered the sun. The wind was whipping across the sea, not agreeing with the water as it swirled higher and higher before it hit the shore.

"Ahem." I cleared my throat, pulled my shoulders back, and gave a hard knock on the lighthouse door.

"Violet." Darren looked a little taken aback when he swung the door open and saw me standing there. "What are you doing here?"

I tried not to get lost in his mussed-up dark hair, amazing thick brows, and chocolate eyes. My heart twirled around like the mirror ball I was sure would be hung over the dance floor at the Sparkle Ball.

I gulped.

"We have some business to take care of. Remember?" I took a step forward to go inside, but he moved a step closer, blocking me.

"Yeah. I'm sorry. It was late when I got home last night, and I will be by tonight." He kept his hand on the door and pulled it closer to his back, closing it off to the inside.

"About that." I was going to give him the little bit of information about my parents hearing his sneaking in the gate, which meant he wasn't so sneaky, but that changed.

"The coffee smells so good," a woman said from inside, behind Darren. "What's going on?"

All of a sudden, Fern Banks pulled the door open from Darren, and her wide-eyed innocence of seeing me standing there was merely a smokescreen. "Hi, Violet. What are you doing here?" She pulled the door open a little more. A towel was wrapped around her body, and another one was curled upon her head, as if she'd just taken a shower.

I pinched my lips together because I didn't want to say something I would regret.

"I see you're busy. We can discuss the little business we have later." I sucked in a deep breath and turned back around.

Oh my gosh. My head started to hurt.

"I can't believe this," I muttered and stormed back up the sidewalk, hoping the once-cold air would cool off my heated body. "I can be the Merry Maker without him. I just need to find a way." I stomped harder and harder, so deep into my own thoughts that I didn't hear Darren running up behind me.

He laid his hand on my shoulder, stopping me dead in my tracks next to the fountain.

"Violet. Stop," Darren said.

I shrugged his hand off my shoulder but kept walking.

"Slow down. Please slow down. You've got it all wrong," he said.

I continued to face forward and picked up the pace. I needed people around so he'd stop talking. Or at least so I wouldn't say something out of school, as Mama would say. That meant saying something inappropriate that I'd regret later.

"Really?" Darren stopped shy of the Welcome Center.

"Really!" I blurted out and pulled the door open.

The Welcome Center was a large open room with the village display smack-dab in the middle. It wasn't a little building, and it wasn't a small miniature village of Holiday Junction. In fact, there was a sidewalk for you to walk through the tiny town and take it all in.

"Just because no one is in here at the moment doesn't mean I'm going to talk to you," I told him when we walked past the cute miniature display of Jubilee Inn, which showed Mayor Paisley, the Boston terrier, sitting on the stoop of the inn and having her photo taken with tourists.

A true-to-life activity that looked to be Kristine's addition to this year as the judge.

It was so neat to see the miniature villages and all the objects that represented them. There was a coffee on the roof of the Brewing Beans. The tiny dress in front of the Bubbly Boutique was very cute. Each shop in town was represented. There were so many details it was hard to take them all in.

"It's not what you think." Darren had tried to make it around me, but the walk was so narrow he might knock something down, like a giant.

"It's not?" I gasped. My eyes traveled to one of the new additions, a tall castle with a window at the top. I guessed it was the nursery rhyme "Rapunzel" because Hillary Stevens was propped up against the castle. Her hair was knotted around it, and what appeared to be blood was coming out of her side.

CHAPTER FIVE

"**P**oor girl." I overheard a few people talking about Hillary after Darren and I were ushered outside. "She loved the miniatures so much."

As I stood in the Welcome Center's snow-blanketed yard, the crisp mountain air filled my lungs. The snow-covered peaks of the mountains loomed in the distance, casting a stark contrast against the clear blue sky.

But as I took in the breathtaking scenery, my mind returned to the grisly images I'd seen.

Hillary's body lying on the floor, her back against the castle, her hair tied in a knot around it so the world could see her eyes were wide open, staring blankly at the mini-village she'd tormented on so many occasions. A small pool of blood had begun to trickle on the mini-village floor around her from the wound on her side.

The killer must've been in a fit of rage to have inflicted such a wound and taken the time to tie her up by her own hair.

I shivered as I realized that the murderer could still be lurking nearby, and I made a mental note to stay vigilant as the authorities were inside. The tranquility of the mountain setting was shattered by the violent crime that had taken place here, and I couldn't help but ponder what a tragic end the Village met as the year drew to a close.

"Excuse me." The journalist side of me kicked in. "Did you know her?" I asked the lady.

"Oh, yes. She loved coming in here—well, trespassing." The woman snickered.

"She would trespass?" I asked to coax her a little further.

"Yes." The lady raised her gloved hand to her parka jacket. "But that doesn't mean she deserved this."

"Of course not." I shook my head. I continued, "Why would she trespass?"

Darren Strickland was still next to me. I was doing all I could to avoid eye contact—or contact any sort of–with him.

"She loved to come when the Welcome Center was closed. She would rearrange miniatures in the funniest ways." Again, the lady smiled, but her expression quickly faded away as her brows knitted. "When she destroyed them was when I recognized immediately she'd broken in."

"Broke in?" I asked, knowing the act alone was much different from trespassing, though both were illegal.

"It's not like the locks on the doors are state-of-the-art." She wiggled her shoulders. "They're years old."

"It sounds like you're making excuses for her." It was just my observation. Darren made a coughing noise that wasn't from a real cough. He was trying to tell me something, but I turned my body ever so slightly away from him.

"No, I'm not," she responded with a snippy tone. "I went to her family many times. They said they didn't have time to fool with their adult daughter and her shenanigans."

"Can you tell me where they live?" I asked, just in case I decided to write an article in the *Junction Journal* about it.

"They live off Holly Street, but really, they live at Cup of Cheer." I'd heard the name of the local tea shop, but since I wasn't a big tea drinker, I'd never gone in there before. "They own it. Always working."

"That's why the poor girl never had any rules," another woman commented. Both nodded.

"Look." The lady who worked at the Welcome Center pointed out Chief Strickland and Curtis Robinson, the coroner, who had walked out of the building. "Maybe they are finished and I can get in there and clean up."

"Can I stop by later if I have any more questions?" I asked. I pulled out one of my business cards I kept in my coat pocket just for instances like this and gave it to her.

"Violet Rhinehammer." She made my name sound like it was poison. "I heard you found Hillary. Is that true?"

"Um…" My mouth dried, and I found it hard to swallow at the look on her face. The one that told me she knew I'd found a few bodies since I'd moved to Holiday Junction. "Darren Strickland and I."

Sue me. It was convenient to pull him in when I was being accused of something, and by the way these two women were looking at me, they were judging me.

"I'm sorry to be seeing you like you this, Berta." Darren shook his head. "I mean, Mrs. Bristol."

"I should've known you were involved." Mrs. Bristol scowled at Darren. "Poor Hillary."

"Don't 'poor Hillary' me." Darren's chest puffed out. "She's the one," he started to say.

"I'm sorry, but we need to go. It looks like Darren's father wants to see us." I wasn't sure what was going on among Darren, Hillary, and Mrs. Bristol, but I did know there was some history that I would have to get out of him.

And when Curtis pointed at us, and I saw Chief Strickland make eye contact with me, that was a good excuse to leave without getting any confirmation of whether Mrs. Bristol would talk to me if I needed to come back.

By the way she was eyeballing Darren, I was pretty sure I would have to check out exactly her side of whatever story she had about Hillary and Darren.

"So, are you going to tell me what that was about?" I murmured out of the side of my mouth while Darren and I made our way through the crowd, who'd obviously shown up because they'd heard what'd happened, to get to Chief Strickland.

While Darren told me the story, I couldn't help but notice all the shoe tracks in the snow created by the police department and the locals. The sight immediately made me sick to my stomach. Any and all evidence they might've been able to collect from shoe prints in the snow was tainted.

"Hillary wanted to work at the jiggle joint." Darren's voice brought me out of the possibility of the tainted evidence.

"Jiggle joint." I giggled. It was funny how Darren had started to call his bar with literally no name the jiggle joint.

"The bar." He acted as if I didn't know what he was talking about. He gave a quick shake of his head and continued. "She was a friend. I didn't want to see her wiggling up there, even though we keep it clean. You know I get some stragglers in there from out of town that catcall and all that. I told her she could come in and clean up when the bar wasn't open. Give her a job, something to do so she'd stop going around town and causing trouble."

"Saint Darren. Just helping everyone out." I threw my hands up in the air.

"What is that supposed to mean?" He spat and shoved past me.

"I think you like saving poor lost souls." The heat in my body was rising. My face felt like it was on fire. "Take me, for instance." I stumbled, trying to get closer to him as I whispered, "Merry Maker."

"Ha!" he proclaimed and threw his head back but didn't stop walking. In fact, I thought he picked up the pace. "If I didn't step up to help you, then you'd have failed. You aren't from here. You didn't know the history."

Though he was right about that, I wasn't going to give in.

"Hillary. Obviously, you wanted to help her out. Darren the knight in shining armor for all the ladies," I mocked in a nasty tone.

He continued to laugh which just made me even madder.

"Fine. Fern Banks. Did she break a nail and come running to you?" I asked about the local beauty queen who'd given me grief the day I walked out of the Holiday Junction Airport.

But it worked. That made him stop walking and turn around right before we made it to the front of the crowd.

"That's so cute." He jerked around. My eyes froze on him, and I took in how his massive shoulders filled the coat he wore. He had a powerful set of shoulders that'd been nice to lean on a few times when I was unsure about my place in Holiday Junction.

"What?" My eyes narrowed, and my jaw clenched.

"You're mad." His smooth olive skin stretched over his high cheek-bones when he smiled.

"I'm not mad," I insisted.

"Then you're jealous." His words made me want to slap the hand-someness right off his face.

"I'm not jealous!" I yelled, taking a step forward and knocking his arm with my shoulder, since I was shorter than him.

"Let's just say that you're pretty pale, and the color on your face looks like it could be a big shiny bright-red Christmas ornament." His laughter hit me at my core. "Not a shiny gleaming mirror ball."

Maybe I was a smidge jealous. It was his strong shoulders that made me feel safe. I'd never admit it.

"What's going on with you two?" Chief Matthew Strickland asked. His eyes shifted between Darren and me. "It doesn't seem like it's about this." He pointed back at the building. "So get it out of your head so we can get your statement about Hillary."

"Fine." Darren shoved his hands in the pockets of his coat.

"Fine," I mocked and crossed my arms across my chest.

"Fine," Matthew said, mocking us back. "Darren, you come with me, and Curtis will talk to Violet."

"Why are we being separated?" I asked, totally forgetting about the little tiff because I was feeling slightly uncomfortable and didn't like to linger in that emotional state.

"We can go inside." Curtis held the door open.

Matthew didn't answer my question. He took Darren into a different door.

"We meet again." I wanted to break the ice and get out of my head. The only way I knew to do that was throw on my journalist attitude. "Hillary Stevens, huh? Do you think she broke in and someone caught her?"

Curtis just kept walking.

I kept on peppering him with questions. "Mrs. Bristol mentioned Hillary trespassed a lot. Not only did she rearrange some of the mini-villages, but she also broke a few of them. Who had the Rapunzel theme for this year's entry? I think that's the first person we need to look at and find what possible motive they'd have to kill Hillary."

"Look." Curtis finally sat down on a bench about fifteen feet from where I'd found the body. "I'm just trying to get your statement. If you saw anyone, anything, because Matthew has his hands full. Some of the town council members have already shown up and in so many words told Matthew to get this solved and tidied up before the stroke of midnight on New Year's Eve."

"That's ridiculous." I snorted. "That's in a couple of days."

"Which is why I'm taking your statement. To help out." Curtis opened the door just enough for me to see an opportunity.

Mae West. She loved to snoop and solve this kind of murder-y stuff. That would keep her busy while I did my Merry Maker duties.

It was a perfect plan.

"Hold on right there," I said. "I know someone who'd be more than happy to help out in the investigation department." I pulled my phone out of my pocket. "Not only is she a smart person with a lot of resources, but she's also fast."

Curtis was about to protest. I'd already dialed Mae's number, and she answered right away.

"Why on earth did you leave me with your mother?" There was a little anger in her voice.

"Don't worry. Your trip to Holiday Junction just got very interesting." I sucked in a deep breath. "There's a dead body, and I need you to help me solve the case."

"Thank goodness!" Was it wrong that Mae sounded excited? "I was about to blow this sleepy village!"

CHAPTER SIX

"Why are you bringing me here?" Mae skipped alongside of me on our way to Cup of Cheer, the shop Hillary Stevens's parents owned. "I would much rather go back to Brewing Beans, where Millie Kay took me."

"This is the shop Hillary Stevens's parents owned." I wasn't sure what the plan was at the moment, but I felt like I needed to go there.

"Don't you think they are at home mourning the loss of their daughter?" Mae asked.

"Yes, which was why I thought we could go there and possibly question the staff about Hillary and her parents." I pulled that one out of my hat.

"That's a pretty good idea, actually," Mae agreed, though I didn't dare tell her that I just came up with it, so I rolled on with the idea.

"I can tell them I'm here from the *Junction Journal* and do an interview-style line of questioning." I continued to talk and took in the decorations the Village Council had put up for the upcoming Sparkle Ball. "Oh my gosh," I gasped.

A huge steel structure outline of some sort of person was erected in the middle of Holiday Park. The structure stood next to the fountain that wasn't there when I'd passed by on my way to the Welcome Center.

People were stringing what looked like large white-bulbed lights to outline the attraction.

"What?" Mae asked. "Did you think of something?"

"Hold on a minute." I dragged her along with me toward the fountain. We had to move around a few of the new displays they'd also put out.

THE POINSETTIA PLANTS that were in the large pots during Christmas were replaced by glittery disco-style balls along with gold fountain-type stringy sparkles.

"Excuse me." I had to speak a little louder to be heard over the rumble of all the chatter as people continued to string the lights around the structure. "What is this?"

Mae decided to wander over to another group of people, no doubt checking out what they were doing.

"The Merry Maker countdown to the new year." The man pointed out at what I could see now was the steel outline of a person, with no gender markings but a shirt with every single possible holiday marker.

There was a four-leaf clover, Christmas bell, flower, bunny, turkey, and many more symbols that were also getting their fair share of string lights wrapped around them.

"You know." The man must've seen the confusion on my face. "The Merry Maker is the—"

I stopped him.

"Yeah. I know what the Merry Maker is, but I didn't realize you did this to mark a new year." If he'd thought I was confused, he was right.

"New York City drops the big ball at the stroke of midnight." He snickered. "We drop the Merry Maker."

"Oh." My brows lifted, and slowly I nodded, realizing there was so much more to this town that I had no clue about. "Thanks."

I excused myself and let him go back to stringing the lights. I found Mae next to the fountain, where she was wrapping up a conversation she was having.

"Ready?" I asked and greeted the other person with a simple smile.

"Sure," Mae said. "It was nice meeting y'all. Happy New Year," she told the group she'd just met.

"So?" she asked when we started back on our journey down toward the path leading to the seaside where we'd find Cup of Cheer.

"So what?" I had been so lost in my thoughts about the Merry Maker drop at midnight that I'd not heard all of Mae's question.

"Did the guy you were talking to give you any information on Hillary?" she asked.

"Hillary?" I shook my head. "No. No. I was asking about the Merry Maker."

"What is that?" Mae's head jerked around. "I've heard that term so many times from the group back there."

"The Merry Maker is supposed to be this festive secret job who marks the end of the holiday by placing a large sign-type structure to identify where the last hurrah of the holiday will take place." I knew I wasn't explaining it very well. "See right there next to the lighthouse?"

Inwardly, I groaned as we walked past. Images of Fern Banks standing at the door from a few hours ago recurred in my mind.

"The Merry Maker put a sign there for the last-night events for the big Halloweenie celebration back in October. The Merry Maker picks the spot, and residents find the sign and gather there the last night of each holiday." All of a sudden, my heart felt a warm fondness for the task I'd been given as the Merry Maker that'd not been there before. "Really, it's a cool thing. No one knows who the Merry Maker is because it's all done in the middle of the night."

"Middle of the night, huh?" Mae's tone made me jerk around to look at her, nearly tripping over the curb of the sidewalk.

"What does that mean?" I asked. I should've just kept my mouth shut.

"Why didn't you tell me you were the Merry Maker?" Mae asked.

"What are you talking about?" I scoffed and brushed off her question like it was ridiculous.

"You're the Merry Maker. I can see it in your face." She pointed with a smile. "Why else would Millie Kay tell me all about Darren Strickland sneaking in and out of the gate to your garage apartment only during the holidays?"

"That's silly." I didn't deny it, but I didn't tell the truth either. "We need to get our heads fixated on who would do such a thing to Hillary."

"Gail Steinner." Mae sternly said the name of someone I didn't even know.

"Who?" I asked and tucked my chin when I saw Darren Strickland rushing toward us from the direction of the jiggle joint. I veered my body left, forcing Mae to step off the curb and head toward the beach.

"Gail Steinner is the person who added the Rapunzel piece to this year's mini-village entry." Mae's words fell off when I heard Darren yelling my name. She turned over her shoulder. "That man, the good-looking one, is yelling for you."

"He's nobody." After I heard his footsteps getting closer, I picked up the pace.

"He's a cute somebody." Mae continued to gawk behind her. "Oh my goodness. That's Darren Strickland."

She abruptly stopped in the middle of the street.

"And you're ignoring him." Her face slid to look at me, and her mouth gaped open with a slight smile. "What are you hiding, Violet Rhinehammer?"

"Hey." Darren huffed and puffed, having caught up to us. "You must be Mae West. Darren," he said, starting to introduce himself.

"Strickland." His last name dripped out of Mae's mouth in her slow Southern accent. "It's so good to finally put a face to a name. You little gate sneaker."

She gave him a light punch on his arm.

"Gate sneaker?" Curiosity settled on his face.

"The Merry Maker thing." Mae wagged her finger between Darren and me.

"You..." He was about to talk about it.

"I have no idea why she thinks I'm the Merry Maker." I rolled my eyes. "If you'll excuse us, I'm trying to spend as much time with my friend while she's here for the Sparkle Ball. I'm going to be so busy that I won't have time for anything else."

"You mean you're part of the Merry Maker deal you two have going." Mae was not letting up.

"No. That's silly," I said, continuing to play it off. "I don't want to be bothered by anything new at the paper."

"We are going to Cup of Cheer to look into Hillary's murder." Mae kept feeding Darren's need to know what I was doing.

"That's because you love to sleuth and I love to…" I sucked in a deep breath, unable to find the words.

"What's this business about being a gate sneaker?" Darren asked Mae. I opened my mouth. He turned to me. "I'm not talking to you."

"Darren Strickland, I like you." Mae grinned. "Not too many people give Violet Rhinehammer a run for her money or put the little look in her eye."

"I am responsible for it." Darren's melancholy grin flitted across his features. "But it doesn't explain the gate sneaker."

"I'm not listening to you two." I plugged my ears with my fingers and started to walk away. "Lalala. I'm not listening."

The two followed me closely enough for me to hear if I barely held my fingers up to my ears as though they were closed.

"Millie Kay informed me how you love to sneak into the gate late at night but only during the holiday. Which made me think you two were the famous Merry Maker, though it was only supposed to be one person." I heard Mae clearly giving her theory. "Since Violet is a new resident, she probably doesn't know all the history of the Merry Maker, and let's just call it for what it is. Look at her. She's scrawny, and I can't imagine she'd be able to lift something like a big Merry Maker sign all over town."

"And that's why Violet says you're good at solving crimes." Darren pretty much told her that her theory was true. "Which means you can help Violet and me find out who killed Hillary Stevens."

"I thought that was what we were doing." They talked as though I weren't there.

"Why would you dare encourage him?" I asked her.

"Because if you don't light the spark between you two, then I will."

My jaw tightened. My eyes grew as big as the smile on Darren's face.

There was a spark? Great. Now I was stuck with her words tattooed on my brain.

CHAPTER SEVEN

There was no sense in correcting Mae on her observation and no time to do it. I'd do everything in my power to try to convince her later that her observation was wrong, even though she was spot-on. We were on a mission to get to Cup of Cheer before Darren's father did, and he was all too eager to go with us.

Once I told her about Fern Banks, our history, and how I'd caught her at Darren's lighthouse, I was sure Mae would see my side of things.

Who knew so many people loved tea? I thought as soon as we opened the door to the quaint shop where every single table was taken. The chatter among the customers all vibrated together, and I heard little bits of Hillary's name sputtered out as we made our way to the tea bar.

One wall had hooks all over it, like hundreds. Each hook had a different mug hanging from its handle. No two mugs were alike, which made it look like a very cool piece of art.

The tables weren't even full tables. They were tray tables. The kind Mama and Daddy would let me eat off when I was sick. The fond memories of the comfort I felt when I ate off one was nostalgic because it was the only time Mama didn't expect me to sit at the dinner table with them.

There were also large leather conversation chairs grouped in twos or threes, where larger parties could gather.

When I looked at the long wooden drawer bar along the opposite wall, I noticed it was only stocked with various teas and small glass pots.

"Welcome to Cup of Cheer." The young woman behind the counter tried to greet us with an upbeat attitude, but the downturn of the edges of her eyes told a different story. "Hi, Darren."

"Prudence, good to see you again." His head tilted, and he offered a faint smile as if he were commiserating with her. "I'm so sorry to hear about Hillary."

"The family is devasted." Prudence slowly shook her head. "They tried to tell Hillary that she needed to keep her opinions to herself."

"Did she have opinions?" I used my shoulder to sort of shove Darren out of the way. When I noticed her hesitation as she looked at me, I corrected myself. "I'm Violet Rhinehammer. I work with Darren's mom at the *Junction Journal*."

"I don't have any comments." Prudence's lips tightened.

"But don't you want to see her killer brought to justice?" I reverted to the days when I was stalking around my own hometown to help get the latest scoop on a murder.

"That's what Chief Strickland is for." She gave me a blank stare with her monotone voice. "What can I get you?"

"I'll have a black coffee with a scone or something sweet." Mae sidled up to the counter.

"I'm sorry, we don't have coffee or sweets. We are strictly a tea shop." Prudence's sad demeanor turned sour fast. "I'm guessing Darren didn't tell you that."

"I'm here for the New Year's Mirror Ball tea." Darren patted his chest. He glanced at me and Mae and held up three fingers. "Make it three."

"I'm not a big fan of—" Mae started to say, but in her style, she turned it around like I'd seen her do so many times before. "I think I will try it. I'm here visiting, and if Darren likes it, I think I will too." She leaned over and whispered to Prudence. "After all, he likes Violet, and I do too. I barely know him but trust his judgement."

Prudence slid her gaze at me before she hurried off to create the special tea.

"What was that about?" I had to ask where she was going with this.

If there was one thing I'd gotten really good at knowing about Mae, it was that she never questioned someone like this unless she was trying to gain something. It was kind of like what Mama did when she would do what I called "Southernfy" a situation.

That meant Mama was manipulating someone to get her way, only she did it in such a sweet manner that the other person had no idea they'd just agreed to do something exactly how Mama wanted it done.

Mae West was the same way.

"Just go with it," Mae said out of the side of her mouth through the grin on her face. Another thing she was good at.

Me, not so much. I was a trained journalist, and I'd been trained that it was simply best to come out and say it or ask it.

Holiday Junction was proving that what I'd learned wasn't working and that I would have to start going about both my job as the head of the *Junction Journal* and living here a little differently.

Darren had snagged a sitting area with four chairs while we were waiting for the fancy tea Prudence was making us.

"What's this business of you two and the"—Mae wagged her finger and mouthed, "Merry Maker?"

"Shh!" I jerked around to see if anyone was looking at us. "Don't be throwing that around."

"I didn't say it. I mouthed it," Mae said, sounding snarky. "And don't give me the business that you don't have a hankerin' on what I'm talking about."

Darren started to laugh, but Mae continued.

"By your reaction, I can tell you're up to something, Violet Rhinehammer." Mae eased back and crossed her arms.

"No wonder you wanted to come here." I sat back and mimicked her by crossing my arms. "You want to forget about your problems with Ellis and try to give me problems when I've moved away from Normal and started a brand-new life for myself."

At the same time, Mae and I looked at Darren, who practically had tears running down his face from laughing, and said, "What?"

"You two." He pointed with one hand and held his stomach with the other. "I love how your relationship is so…"

"So what?" My jaw hardened. "I don't even want to know." I tried to dismiss him by waving a loose hand.

"No. I want to hear what he was about to say," Mae encouraged him.

"I was saying how I could see why you two didn't get along when you lived in the same town. Two very independent, strong-willed, and strongheaded women who really do have the same morals and ideas when it comes to life, but you two just can't see it." I hated it when Darren made sense.

It made it that much harder for me not to be attracted to him.

"Okay. Then based on your assessment of me, why on earth was Fern Banks at your house practically nakey?" I asked.

"Oh. Really?" Mae's Southern accent dripped with curiosity. "And here I thought you were someone good for Violet. Honey"—Mae wagged her finger back and forth, directly staring at Darren—"as my good friend Dottie would say, I think you're slicker than pig snot on a radiator."

"What?" Darren looked stunned for a hot second before he started laughing again.

"Violet, let's go." Mae popped up to her feet. "I think you're right about this one."

"Wait a second." Darren put both hands up. "That's a compliment. You two really are passionate about many things like friendship, doing the right thing, solving murders…" He let the last word linger.

He obviously knew Mae and I loved to stick our noses in murders or at least bring them to justice.

"And if you two keep up this kind of passionate attitude for the next couple of days, I'm sure we can find out who killed Hillary Stevens." He pulled his lips together when Prudence walked up to us with a tray of three cups of tea.

"Did you say you were trying to find the killer?" she asked, easing down into the fourth, available chair. She rested the tray in her lap.

"Thank you." Mae took one of the teacups and handed it to me then took the other for herself. Darren had to get his own. "We were just talking. That's all."

"Do you know something?" I ignored Mae's attempt to get Prudence out of our conversation. "Because I have contacts on getting some solid information to help Chief Strickland with some motives and clues."

"Well..." Prudence hesitated, folded her hands, and placed them on the center of the empty tray. "She really was a sweet girl—woman," she corrected herself, "who only wanted life to remain as it was when she was a child."

"I can relate," I mumbled, thinking about the mishap of my parents thinking they were headed for divorce. The entire last few months' feeling reverberated along the nerves in my body and made me a little sick to my stomach.

I took a sip of tea since I'd heard tea could help soothe a belly.

"Mmm." I licked my lips. "This is delicious. You might've turned me into a tea drinker."

"I told you." Darren gave a hard nod and sat back to enjoy his cup.

"Hillary was always complaining about the mini-village. Especially this time of the year. She didn't want people to add on to it. Heck, when the Village Council decided to add more of the budget to tourism, she stood outside the courthouse and protested with a sign in each hand." Prudence's thin lips told of the emotional roller coaster she was on.

"Do you know anyone on the Village Council who might've had a motive for Hillary not to be around?" That was my way of nicely getting her to call someone out.

"Berta Bristol," she said, referring to the Welcome Center worker.

"She's on the village council?" Mae asked so we could confirm.

"She is," Darren said. "I voted for her."

"I know Berta had mentioned earlier that Hillary came in a lot and did mess things up, but she wasn't overly upset about those incidents." Mae's eyes darted between us.

"Berta sure did let the Stevenses know. It was monthly that Hillary would break into the Welcome Center. Sure enough, Berta would storm in here and raise all sorts of madness."

"A big hissy fit," Mae said and nodded.

"Mm-hmm," I hummed. Both of us knew when someone threw a hissy, they were primed to be out of their minds and do things they'd never do while calm, which made a good headspace for murder.

"What did the Stevenses do?" I asked because I wanted to know exactly how they handled an adult daughter. "It's not like they can control Hillary."

"Oh, they can. Hillary has never been able to hold down a job. They pay for her house and all her living expenses. They told her if she didn't stop acting out and didn't get a real job, they were going to have to cut her off." Prudence was privy to all sorts of juicy gossip.

Even though this information didn't pertain to Hillary's death, it was very interesting to hear.

"Just a few weeks ago, Berta came in and pretty much warned them that if they didn't keep a close eye on Hillary during the mini-village contest coming up"—Prudence was referring to the event now—"she was going to have to take action to make Hillary's craziness stop."

"Did she say what kind of action?" I asked, since it sounded an awful lot like Berta had just threatened the Stevenses if not Hillary herself, which would give Berta the real motive and actions of a killer.

"No. She just said she'd take Hillary into her own hands if they couldn't." Prudence looked down and then away as if she suddenly realized the severity of these words. She jumped to her feet. "I've said too much."

"Thank you," I told her. "We will check all this out and not say a word about who told us."

"I'd appreciate that." Prudence hurried off with the tray underneath her arm.

"Think about it. Berta has all access to the building." I leaned over with the cup in between both hands. In a hushed voice, I said, "Day or night. She said she's there day and night, especially now. There were no cameras, so she knew she'd not be seen." I recalled what Berta had told me.

"Did you notice how none of the mini-village was messed up? It was untouched, as if Hillary had been killed somewhere else and then placed." Darren had a keen eye that I'd not picked up on.

"If someone was trying to tie me up by my hair…" I gulped and took a fistful of hair to dangle over my right shoulder. "I'd fight tooth and nail."

"And the Rapunzel castle didn't look messed up at all." Darren's words made me shiver.

Not even sitting in front of the Cup of Cheer fireplace was going to make those goose bumps go away. The only thing that would make that happen was going back and talking to Berta.

CHAPTER EIGHT

Of course, Mae couldn't just leave it at Berta. She continued to play that "what if Berta wasn't the killer?" game.

"Think about it," Mae said as we took Darren up on his offer to head to the jiggle joint so he could check in on his bar while we continued to put our heads together.

"Maybe the killer wants everyone to believe Berta did it. She'd have the most obvious reason, and the threat Prudence claimed Berta made was in public. Anyone in there could've overheard, and it was their time to do the deed." Mae stopped talking as soon as we stepped into the bar.

"This is a real jiggle joint," she whispered into my ear and noticed the girl on the stage dancing underneath the mirror ball. "And I'm assuming this isn't where the Sparkle Ball is going to take place."

"I run a clean jiggle joint." Darren shrugged. "Clothes on, clean music. I have morals."

"Yeah." Mae snorted on our way to the open barstools butted up to the counter. Darren headed toward the back.

"Mae, I'd like you to meet the Easter Bunny and the Tooth Fairy." I pointed at Shawn and Owen.

"Then you should remember the nasty letter I sent you when I was five. You stopped giving me any money for these pearly whites." Mae opened her mouth and showed him her teeth.

"She does know I'm not the real Tooth Fairy, right?" Shawn teased. "I like you." He grinned. "Darren, get this gal a drink on me."

"I'll have a beer." Mae was such a good sport.

"Shawn." He stuck his hand across my front since I was sitting between the two.

"Mae." She took it. "I'm a friend of Violet's from home."

When it was apparent the two of them were going to carry on a conversation, I switched seats with her.

While the three of them were busy telling stories and laughing, I decided to take the free time to talk to Darren in code about the Merry Maker job.

"Obviously, we still have to do what we said we would." In not so many words, I was letting him know that though he had some sort of tryst with Fern, I was willing to overlook it so we could get the job done. "So just tell me what you're thinking for the final."

I didn't have to say "the final destination for the New Year's holiday" because he was smart enough to read between the lines.

"I was thinking Cup of Cheer." He reached down into the ice chest and took out three beers, uncapped them, and placed them in front of Mae, Shawn, and Owen. "They can keep drinking while we figure this out."

"Why there?" I wondered.

"I think it would be nice for the family to have a gathering of support. I've known them my whole life, and..." He stopped and gulped. "Let's just say I owe them."

"Owe them?" I knew this had something to do with the Stricklands' history.

Ever since I moved to Holiday Junction, I'd seen an underlying tension between the cousins, Darren, and Rhett, that told me something was going on that was, as we'd say in Kentucky, swept under the rug.

Boy, was I good at that. I could smell it a mile away.

"It was one of those things when we were in high school." Darren wiped down the counter with the rag and tossed it back when he was done.

"You and Hillary went to high school together?" I was thinking she was younger because of her childlike activities and the way she dressed.

"Yes. I went to school here." Darren snickered.

"I know that, but she doesn't…" I searched for the words. "I guess I thought she was younger."

Someone's cell phone sang a tune. With my forearms on the edge of the bar, I leaned over and glanced down the line. Mae had her phone in her hand, and she used the other hand to swivel the barstool around. Then she excused herself to take the call. She didn't even glance at me when she walked past and outside, where there were fewer distractions than what was happening in the bar.

"That's kinda why they owe me. She never had a real formal date to any of the events. One day, I was in the tearoom getting some gifts for my mom's birthday, and it was around the time of a school dance." I knew where this tale was going, but I let him continue. "I ended up taking her to a dance. I didn't even think about it when they asked. They paid me fifty bucks, and a moped can get a lot of gas on fifty bucks."

"You took money from them to take out their daughter?" I was beyond mortified.

"It wasn't really like that. It was more like 'here's fifty dollars to use to get her a corsage, take her to supper, and all that,' but I went so low-key on the whole thing, I pocketed most of it." He shrugged, and my stomach lurched at the thought. "What? Don't look so high and mighty. We actually had a really great time. She's super smart and funny, but she had these crazy, way-out-there ideas, and honestly, she should've never gone with me. She should've gone with Troy Kenner."

"The pottery people's son?" The name of the woman who owned the pottery store escaped me.

"Denise Kenner." Darren nodded. "Anyways, Troy and Hillary started talking at the dance, and truly, they were so like-minded that I could've walked away and they'd never know because they were so wrapped up in their conversation."

"Why didn't you just leave?" I wondered why he would stay at the dance.

"I was afraid her parents were going to want the fifty dollars back." His lips turned wry. My heart flipped, and I had to look away. "What are you thinking?"

"Huh?" I asked, trying not to stare directly into his eyes. He fixed a glass of ice water. Then he put down a paper napkin in front of me and set the glass on top.

"You looked away like you were thinking something." He did seem to notice the subtle shifts in my body language.

"What happened to Denise's son, Troy?" I asked.

"There was talk around town after that about Troy and Hillary. Like a couple." Instead of just standing there and talking to me, Darren had to fidget with something. He picked up a glass off the drying rack and started to dry the vessel with a towel. "Her parents were so happy about it. Told me it was the best fifty bucks they'd ever spent. For some reason, they thought I was the matchmaker."

"That's a little sad." I picked at the corner of the paper napkin. "What happened to Troy?"

"His family was a different story once they found out he wanted to stay in Holiday Junction instead of going out into the world to learn about pottery so he could take over Ceramic Celebration." Darren had no idea he just revealed a motive for Denise to have killed Hillary. "He still works there, but I don't think he and Hillary talked too much after his mom went a little off the rails about things."

"Darren." I gasped and smacked the top of the counter. "We have a motive. The Stevenses owe you more than a favor." I had an offbeat idea. "What if we go see them and you suggest we look into things? Get them to tell us what they think or who they think killed their daughter. Maybe see if they think Denise Kenner held some sort of hard feelings about her son not going away." I gulped and recalled what Louise had said earlier. I jutted my finger at him. "Your own mother said Denise told her or something like that." I knew this was how rumors got started, but still I was on too much of a roll to even stop to recall exactly what Louise had mentioned. I backtracked. "Denise said something about Hillary coming into the Ceramic Celebration and just destroying the place."

"Destroying?" He questioned the bold word.

"Maybe not destroy the whole place, but from what I understood, she did some damage." I grabbed the glass and took a sip, staring at him over the rim.

His eyes narrowed when he looked at me. Not the type of stare in which he was actually seeing me. More of the kind that indicated thinking, with a very subtle nod.

Somehow, I felt mentioning their daughter would make it more personal for them and they'd do it.

Darren's eyes held a hint of hesitation.

"They must trust you if they asked you to take her to the dance." I encouraged him to agree. "I don't know if Denise or Troy had anything to do with it, but from what I gather from you about Hillary's history, she wasn't close to too many people. Those are the people who might understand why Hillary did what she did and, like you, just gave us a couple of more suspects to look at."

"Yeah." He hurried off in the direction of one of his employees and mumbled something to them before he walked around the bar to me. "What are you waiting for? We have some pottery to make, and we have to go see Vern." He grabbed my hand and tugged me.

Quickly, I jerked it away.

"Listen, Violet." Before I knew what was happening, he wrapped his hand around the back of my neck, pulled me to him, and planted a big kiss on my lips.

I wanted to pull away, but it would be rude. Even Mama would get on me for having bad manners. At least that was what I told myself, finally giving in a little to the kiss.

"If that doesn't tell you that nothing happened between Fern Banks and me, then nothing will." He smiled and winked. "And you didn't pull away."

The sound of clapping echoed around us.

When I turned around to see who it was, I could feel Darren's breath on the back of my neck, he was standing so close.

"It's about dang time," Owen said and clapped in time with Shawn.

CHAPTER NINE

"What was that back there?" I couldn't leave well enough alone. It was like our Southern saying back home about beating a dead horse, only I couldn't just beat it—I had to drive a truck over it, put the vehicle in reverse, and do it all over again a few times until I was exhausted mentally and physically thinking and talking about it.

"That was my bar, the one you call the jiggle joint." Darren snorted and led the way down the sidewalk to the seaside ceramic shop. "You know, the name is starting to stick. Instead of calling it Bar, I might change the name."

"That's the most ridiculous thing I've ever heard." I jerked around when I suddenly realized Mae wasn't around. "Where did Mae go?"

"Beats me." He wagged a finger at me and then at the door of the jiggle joint. "I thought you were trying to get rid of her earlier."

"I was, but I was trying to pawn her off on someone else, not just let her go off in a strange town by herself." I gnawed on my lip and then got a little taste of the lingering kiss I'd experienced.

"Do you need to go find her?" he asked. "We don't have time to go find her, check out Ceramic Celebration, and then go see Vern before we go to my parents' for the dinner."

"The dinner." I smacked the palm of my hand on my forehead. "I forgot all about it."

"I made you forget a lot of things." He boldly took credit for giving me a kiss that made me blank out. "I've got a power pucker." He made kissing noises. "Plus, it got you to stop talking in there."

"You kissed me to stop my talking?" I stomped and lowered my eyes.

"No. I kissed you because I had to get Fern Banks out of your head." He zipped up his coat. With the sun starting to go down, the winter wind whipped off the ocean more than usual. "Fern was at the jiggle joint last night after tying one on."

"You should've stopped serving her." I decided to go to the pottery shop and restarted our journey, which was only a few shops away.

"I didn't serve her. She'd been overserved before she even made it to the bar." He put his hands in his coat pocket and kept in step with me. "She'd been at the Village Town Council end-of-year party, and she mentioned something about Troy Kenner and something about having to call my dad about Hillary."

"What did she say?" I wanted to smack Darren for not remembering these little details after seeing Hillary dead.

"It's all coming back to me." He stopped walking in front of Ceramic Celebration's display window. As he talked, I couldn't help but notice the mini-village in the window. "She said Hillary was there and protesting the dollars that were made from the tourism be spent on the party and that they needed to make miniatures of the town council members who were always using the money for themselves. So many random things, but she was drunk, and I knew I couldn't leave her at the bar, so I took her back to the lighthouse, where she slept in the guest bedroom."

He made sure he emphasized the phrase "guest bedroom."

"Look." He pointed at the door of the pottery shop. The sign was flipped to Closed.

"We will have to come back." I looked at the pieces of paper hanging on the door to see if there was a store schedule, but they were just about the upcoming classes for the new year.

A loud noise like someone peeking on glass made me look at the Freedom Diner.

MAMA HAD her nose butted up to the glass and was waving at us to come inside.

Like the rest of the shops and stores in town, the diner was a dingy white clapboard house with a covered front. A banner of strung-together triangles with the American flag hung down along the front, and a small blue sign with Freedom Diner written on it in plain letters hung out from an iron arm. It looked like the Fourth of July all year around at the diner.

A Coca-Cola machine as well as a bagged ice machine sat underneath the covered porch to the door's left. To the right of the diner door were two chairs that didn't match. One was a steel-framed, straight-back chair with a padded leather cushion that had a big crack down the middle. The other was a folded chair with a braided seat used as a picnic chair. Many of the webbed braids were frayed and looked a little dry-rotted. Pretty much anything in the elements of the seaside cottages had seen better days, thanks to the salt erosion, but the effect added to the charm.

Once inside the diner, I saw Mae was with Mama and Daddy. They were seated in the padded chairs at one of the corner acrylic-top tables.

"The bar was all taken up, huh?" I knew Daddy loved coming to sit at the bar with the stools across as he met with his new buddies he'd encountered since moving to Holiday Junction.

"That, and we wanted to talk to Mae about Normal and if anything had changed." Mama was having a good old time catching up on all the latest gossip. "We was talking about Ty Randal losing his mind. He had to've gone crazy to get married to Ellis. Sugar"—Mama reached over and patted Mae's hand—"just 'cause it zips don't mean it fits."

I also noticed the few glass cake stands along the counter. They were filled with plates of delicious pie and cake slices that tickled my taste buds.

"What?" Darren laughed. His eyes twinkled. They always twinkled when he looked at Mama.

"She means that Ellis and Ty, the couple she's talking about, really don't go together." I tried to ignore that he'd pulled out the chair for me to sit in, but it was hard to do because out of the corner of my eye, Mama nudged Mae, who rapidly nodded. "Thanks, Darren," I said in an upbeat, no-big-deal manner.

"It doesn't refer to you two." Mama wiggled her nose.

"Okay, enough." Daddy gave me a sympathetic look. He'd had a front-row seat to how Mama stuck her nose into everything while I was growing up. "I understand you three saw the local gal murdered this morning."

"I was just telling your mama about how we were going to find out who killed Hillary." Mae had the glow of the thrill seeker she'd become. A look I'd seen her develop over the few years we'd both lived in the same town. "With Violet's amazing journalistic instincts and my awesome sleuth skills, we will have it all tied up before the sparkly ball drops at Holiday Park."

"Wow, you thought about this." I shook my head, picked up the table's coffee carafe, and filled up the mug sitting in front of me.

Daddy didn't seem too interested. Once he saw one of his friends walk into the diner, Daddy excused himself and took what was left of his pie up to the counter so he could visit, leaving us at the table to entertain Mama. Or maybe for her to entertain us.

"I was telling Violet about the history I had with Hillary." Darren had gotten the sleuthing bug and eagerly told everyone at the table about Hillary and Troy.

"I wasn't going to say anything, but—" Mama paused as if she were looking for the right words. "When I was making my final pie at Ceramic Celebration, I did see Hillary and Troy outside the window. They were having a heated discussion on the sidewalk. Of course, I wasn't paying all that much attention to it."

Right, I thought.

"I had to get the first layer of paint on the pie to make it right before

I used the lighter brown to paint the lattice on top." Mama yammered on about the decoration before she finally got to the juicy part of what she wanted to say, though she didn't want to make it sound so gossipy. "I'd gotten the red paint from the small little peekaboos of the cherry pie filling under the lattice on my hands."

She stopped, tugged in her lips, and released an audible sigh through her nose.

"I couldn't help but hear what they were fussing about. He said they couldn't meet up because he had to take his life a lot more seriously now. Then he told her that he wasn't going to be able to see her anymore." Mama's lips turned down. "I felt so sorry for the girl. She started to cry, and that was when she told him that she'd destroy anything to do with the pottery shop so he'd be free."

"She said that?" Mae's eyes grew. "You need to write that down." She pointed at me.

"What happened after that?" Darren asked.

"She ran off in such a flurry, I didn't know what to do." Mama's brows knitted, and her lips puckered. A look I knew all too well.

"Mama, you're hiding something." I had to pull whatever it was out of her.

"Well…" She hesitated. "I ran after her."

"You did what?" My jaw dropped.

"Did I stutter?" That was her way of telling me she didn't want to repeat what she'd said.

Darren internally laughed, making him almost spit out his coffee. I stared at him with one brow raised, hoping he'd get the message not to encourage her behavior.

"Honestly, Mother." My jaws clenched. "You need to stop butting into people's business. What if someone saw you talking to her and somehow you became a suspect?"

"Oh, people saw me talking to her. They even saw me walking with her." Mama waved a hand. "I don't give two iotas who saw me doing what. I didn't do anything but tell Hillary what I thought about that boy." She crossed her arms. "Manners."

59

"Here we go again." I pointed a finger at her. "Don't be getting any more of those manner-class ideas."

"If that girl had grown up with some manners about dating, she'd not be where she is right this moment. Dead," she said flatly, like we didn't know. "I'm telling you that boy killed her."

"What did she say to make you think that?" Mae hushed me when I opened my mouth. She was going to try her hand at talking to Mama since her foster mama wasn't too much different from mine.

"She said she and Troy had been secretly dating, and his mother recently found out about it. From what I understand, she nearly took to the bed over it. I told Hillary that he wasn't worth it and once she set her sights on someone who treated her like a lady, she'd be happier than a boll weevil hiding in a tub of grits."

Now that made Darren spit out his coffee.

"What?" Mama asked, as if she didn't know she tickled Darren to his core.

She even winked at him, only making him laugh even more.

"Mama, now is not the time to make jokes. This is very serious." I was annoyed at the whole situation.

"But you've given us a very good clue to go on." Mae tapped her fingernail on the table. "I really think the first suspect is her boyfriend."

"I wouldn't call him that." Mama ran her finger around the edge of her glass. "She didn't call him that. She called him her best friend for life. They made some sort of pact years ago, and apparently, he'd kept it until recently. His mother never liked her, apparently. Something about his throwing his life away. Small town. All those things we mothers say when we want the best for our children."

"What about her parents?" I turned the question on Darren. "Did they ever say anything to you about the Stevenses?"

"No, that was why I wanted to go see them. Maybe get some more insight on not only Troy and his family but others who'd come in and talked to them about Hillary's behavior," he said.

"There is one more thing." Mama had saved the juicy part for last. "When I was leaving, the poor girl kept saying how things were perfect around here before the new Village Council had decided to change everything. She said even the Merry Maker had been acting very different than in years past and that she was going to find out exactly who the Merry Maker was. But she also muttered Fern Banks's name."

Mama's brow ticked up, and she looked at me.

This was the second time Fern Banks's name had been brought up in conjunction with Hillary. It looked like I was going to have to discard that part of the "Auld Lange Syne" line. *Should auld acquaintance be forgot*

And never brought to mind?

Should auld acquaintance be forgot

And the days of auld lang syne?

Because no matter how hard I tried to forget about Fern Banks, she wouldn't go away this time. Not yet, anyway.

Why had I ever agreed to be the Merry Maker? There was no time to waste. If Hillary had even mentioned the Merry Maker to anyone in this town, the Merry Maker would be the next suspect on the list, and I dang sure knew well and good I didn't kill her.

"Seems like someone's in what, at home, Millie Kay would call a pickle." Darren tried his hand at sounding like Mama.

"Listen, if I'm in a sticky situation, you are too." I stomped down the sidewalk, going past the shops so I could make it to the small seaside neighborhood that butted up to the woods. The dead-end street had a path that led us straight to Vern McKenna's shed, located deep in the forest. The shed was secret and held all the ins and outs of the Merry Maker. So whoever found out about the shed would have great insight into the current Merry Maker. That was why it was so important to sneak out of the house after dark—so no one could see my comings and goings anywhere near the woods.

Vern was handy. He had great woodworking skills and was able to make the large wooden holiday structures used for the Merry Maker to mark the holiday's last hurrah. This particular structure would have some sort of symbolism for marking the last day of the year as the town celebrated the year's final holiday.

"You're very quiet." Darren kept up with me as I hurried down the small street.

"Now that we have Mae and Mama going back to Mama's house to get ready for supper at your parents', we have to get to Vern." Time was of the essence. "The investigation will still be there tomorrow, but we have to strategically come up with a plan to see everyone we think might've done it."

The sound of gentle waves lapping against the beach mixed in with the cold blustery wind that beat our backs as we hurried down the little neighborhood. Sights of leftover Christmas decorations butted up against the small cottage homes. Darkness had fallen so early now with the time change that it was hard to tell if it was five p.m. or three a.m.

Televisions playing the evening news glowed from the windows of a few of the houses.

Long gone were the chirping crickets and nocturnal critters who usually scurried around during the warmer months. The leaves were gone from the trees, and the empty limbs climbed high in the sky like scary monsters hovering over us as the dark clouds rapidly danced along the sky as though it was their own personal dance floor.

Darren's phone rang.

"It's my dad." Darren's voice fell. My heart stopped. "Do you think he knows about the Merry Maker? He never calls me."

We stopped shy of the edge of the woods.

"The only way to find out is to answer it." It was a simple suggestion, but I knew it was hard for Darren since he wasn't really close to his father.

Yet another secret I'd need to explore more but not tonight.

"Hey, Dad, what's up?" Darren answered and turned away from me. "Yeah. Mm-hmm. Now? Okay." He paused a few times between his words.

"Well?" I asked when he turned back around and put the phone in the pocket of his jacket.

"Dad wants to see us right now before everyone gets there for dinner." He rocked back on his shoes. "I guess the Merry Maker gig is going to have to wait."

CHAPTER TEN

The trolley had long stopped serving the community, since it only ran during daylight hours. Walking back to town and down the main street to the Strickland compound would take much longer than we needed to get there now, just like Chief Matthew Strickland had demanded, so we only had one option.

Darren's moped.

"The scene of the crime," I muttered, referring to my earlier run-in with Fern Banks.

"Don't be one of those girls." Darren sounded as if I'd already exhausted him with mentioning the local beauty queen's name.

"I'm not one of those girls." I found myself wondering if I was one of those jealous types because he was right. "I am very confident in who I am. Unlike someone I know, I hopped on an airplane to take a chance on not only my career, my friends, and my entire life."

I stood back and watched him unlock the door on the opposite side of the lighthouse, which was a storage room, but he kept his moped in there.

"Something you didn't do." I went to reach for the helmet he had extended for me to wear, but he paused, staring at me like I'd hit a nerve. "Not that you needed to, but..." I wanted to take that back instantly. "I'm sorry. That was low. I have no real idea about your family and your life. I just know that when I'm with you, it's kinda electric, and I don't really know how to deal with that emotion."

"Violet Rhinehammer." He looked down at me, dropping his hands from the strap he'd snugged beneath his chin. Drawing in a slow, steady smile, he said, "Are you falling for me?"

"Stop it." I looked away and busied my hands as I tried to strap the helmet on.

"I'm serious." He put his hands on mine, meaning for me to let go as he finished adjusting the helmet for me. "The kiss a few months ago. The looks across the street when we pass. The kiss tonight."

"I-I..." I gulped, not sure I should tell him that I'd never really had a boyfriend. Dates. Never a boyfriend. "I think we need to go."

"I think I want to discuss this now." The way he looked at me made me think of Mama.

Right about now, she'd say something about him being so hot, she'd bite him on the hiney and pray for lockjaw.

I burst out laughing.

"What?" He rubbed his hand under his nose. "Do I have a hanger?"

"Hanger?" I laughed even louder.

"A booger." He bent down and looked at his reflection in the tiny mirror on the moped's handlebar.

"No." I couldn't stop laughing. I heaved in and out, trying to catch my breath.

"Fine." He jerked the kickstand of the moped and got on. "Get on if you're coming."

"Why are you so mad?" I climbed behind him and noticed he'd not steadied the moped with his feet like he normally did. I wobbled a few times before finally getting situated with my arms snuggled tight around his waist.

"Nothing." He revved up the moped and zoomed off, making it hard for me to talk to him reasonably.

I put my mouth close to his ear and said, "I'm sorry if I hurt your feelings. You make fun of my sayings all the time."

His body tensed underneath my arms. This wasn't the time to address any sort of issues. He made that clear. Instead of worrying about the situation between us, I decided to focus on whatever it was Matthew wanted to talk to us about.

It must've been important because the compound gates slid open as soon as the moped approached the brick wall on this side of the street. The hedges had blankets of white lights and some cut-out gold glittering numbers signaling the numerals of the new year.

The moped zoomed up the drive. The twinkle lights were strung on all the tall trees that stood along each side, giving off all the festive feelings. I was a sucker for the sparkly lights the residents had hung up all over the village to ring in the New Year.

The Stricklands took it even further by decorating the perfectly trimmed shrubs up next to the large family home. Even the hanging egg chair on the porch had a little mirror ball dangling from the top of it. Nothing was off-limits to decorate around the village.

Darren brought the moped to a halt and pushed the kickstand down before he got off. He did give me a hand.

"Thank you." I smiled and unbuckled the helmet strap from underneath my chin.

He didn't say anything or even look at me. He simply dangled our helmets on the handlebars.

"Hey." I put my hand on his arm when he started toward the porch. "I wanted to say something before we went in there."

Slowly, he turned and stared.

"I didn't mean to hurt your feelings. This whole thing"—I pointed at him and then myself—"is all new to me. I've never really dated anyone."

The hit of vulnerability, a feeling I never liked, landed in my stomach.

"I'm not saying we are dating, but the kissing thing, the flirting—"

He put his finger up to my mouth to stop me from talking.

"It's not like I'm some big-time player. Look around. There's not a lot of options in Holiday Junction." His jaw softened, as did the look in his eyes. "What's wrong with hanging out? Taking things slow?"

65

"Yeah. I could be up for that." I gave a nonchalant smirk. "That sounds good. Not complicate things."

"If they don't turn out, then no one will know, and we move on." The front door of the home squeaked open. Our eyes were on each other. "No harm, no foul."

"Right." I nodded.

"Shall we?" He turned and led the charge up the steps of the old family home, which itself should have been some sort of museum to the town. It had more history inside than the Welcome Center.

That was what happened when a family like the Stricklands had lived in Holiday Junction over many generations.

Matthew stood at the door. He wasn't alone. Curtis Robinson was with him.

"We can meet in my office." Matthew didn't waste any time with pleasantries. By the tone of his voice, he was all business and not at all fatherly.

The house smelled like it was suppertime. I couldn't place what Louise and Marge were cooking for supper, but my stomach agreed as it growled to life.

"Don't let him keep you too long." Marge appeared at the end of the entry hallway. She had her usual brown shawl draped over her shoulders. Her neatly styled bobbed hair matched the silver, glittery Happy New Year banner hanging along the wall above the table. The greenery and long-stemmed brass candleholders with gold candles flickered with life.

"Don't worry. We won't." I patted my belly. "Something smells really good."

"It's the Strickland family recipe for beef tenderloin." She smiled and clasped her hands together. "It's passed down to every woman who is a Strickland or becomes a Strickland. Maybe you'll get it one day."

Ahem. Matthew cleared his throat and looked back at me with a hairy brow cocked.

He'd already mentioned that Darren and I seemed to be spending time together. But if only they knew it was all about the Merry Maker. At first.

"Let's not get ahead of ourselves," Matthew told his sister before he shuffled us into the office, where he quickly closed the door behind me, the last one lagging.

"We," he said in a stern voice as he gestured to himself and Curtis, "have come to the conclusion that we are going to need some help solving this murder."

"Hillary was knocked out with chloroform and then placed at the scene. There was no real damage to Hillary's follicles, which tells me she was tied up before she was murdered by a stab wound." Curtis opened the file and laid some crime scene photos on the desk.

Darren looked away with a shiver. I continued to search the photos to see if there was anything I'd previously encountered that might give a clue.

"There were no village pieces tipped over either." I made sure to restate what Mae had noticed when we were at the scene. "So the killer was very meticulous in placement. Do we think it was someone like a man? Strong? Able to place her there?"

Curtis laid down another photo of Hillary on the autopsy table. The one picture that stood out to me was the one zeroed in on the stab wound.

"It's circular. Not a knife," I observed.

"We don't have the murder weapon." Matthew glanced up for a second. "The object was long enough to clip the organs, making Hillary bleed to death as she was passed out on the chloroform."

"At least she didn't seem to suffer." Darren blinked a few times, trying to stop the sad emotions that seemed to course through his body as he thought about his friend. "It seems so drastic to do. Knock her out, put her in an awkward position, and then stab her."

"Personal, son. We'd call this personal." Matthew took a stack of photos and dropped them on top of the autopsy photos. "That's why you're here."

Each photo was a picture from years ago. If I'd not stared into Darren's eyes like I had, I would not have recognized him in the photos.

"Why do you have these out?" Darren asked and gathered them up, but one dropped to the floor.

I picked it up and saw it showed him and Hillary at some sort of prom. Then he snatched it out of my hands.

"What kind of frilly suit is that?" I asked about the sixties- or seventies-looking white tuxedo.

"It was my dad's." Darren shoved the photos into his dad's chest. "Burn those."

"And the hair?" I kept on about the look, going from memory. "I mean, who knew you had so much up top?"

Sure, his hair was still somewhat long and really not a look I'd ever thought was becoming of a man, but it sure did look good on him.

"This was years ago." Darren acted like it wasn't just about ten or so years ago.

"Not that long," I muttered.

"Listen, the point is that you knew her. You two were pretty good friends, from what I recall, and we need you two to just listen around town." Matthew had no idea we were already doing exactly what he was asking. It was just this time, he wanted us to snoop and not scold us for it.

"Let me get this straight." I had to make darn sure that if anyone called him on me for snooping like someone'd done before, he wouldn't threaten to arrest me and throw me in jail. "You want us to sneak around, snoop, and all the things."

"Nothing illegal but what you always do. You know…" I could feel he was about to put me down in his own nice way. "Meddle in other people's business."

"Yes. We can do that." Darren was quick to answer and even faster to get to the door. "Ready? I'm starving."

"Not so fast." I turned to Matthew. "My friend Mae West is in town, as you know. She's really good at talking to people and getting them to talk to her. Will it be okay for me to include her in the investigation?"

"First off, I never said 'investigate.' Just 'meddle.' That's all." Matthew's eyes didn't stray a bit from me as his staring made it very clear I wasn't to put myself in harm's way. "Secondly, if you dare tell anyone I've asked you to do this, not only will we deny it, but we will file some sort of charge against you."

"I'm not a lawyer, but I'm pretty sure this little meeting would make those charges go away. On your end, though, I do understand. I'll just do what I've always done." I flipped my hair over my shoulder and walked over to the closed door, where Darren was still standing. "I'm ready now."

Darren looked back at his father. I wasn't sure if Matthew gave him the go-ahead-and-go look or Darren finally found the confidence he needed to stand up to his dad, but he swung the door open.

Darren led me through the halls, but I noticed the farther away we walked, the more the delicious home-cooked smells were fading.

"Where are we going?" I asked just as he jerked me into what in the shadows appeared to be a bedroom. "Oh, I don't think so. What kind of girl do you think I am?" I protested.

"Relax, princess." He flipped on the lights, and the inside told me this was his childhood bedroom. There weren't any trophies on the wall like I'd seen in Rhett's house. There were a few instruments that weren't out of the ordinary since Darren was in a local band. "I wanted to talk to you about those photos."

"Forget about it. I have some of those too. I just hope Mama left those back at our home in Normal." I made a mental note to be sure I went through the storage boxes stockpiled in Mama's garage and destroy any and all photos of me.

"I wanted to tell you why I asked Hillary to the dance, even though I took the money from her parents." He eased himself on the edge of his bed and patted it for me to sit down next to him. "And why I really want to find her killer."

"Okay. You don't have to." I felt ashamed of myself for even putting him in this position.

"If I don't tell you, and you do stick around Holiday Junction for a

69

while, you're going to find out about everyone's past." His hands rested on his thighs. "Take the photos. You saw how I looked with my big hair, braces, acne, and sense of style."

His own words brought a smile to his face and mine.

"I was in the loser club with Hillary and Troy. When you made fun of me earlier, it put me right back in high school." He made me feel awful for joking about him. "Let me finish."

He was starting to learn my body language and saw I was about to object.

"I never thought of you that way." I had to say something.

"Fine, but Rhett, you see how we are. He was the star of the village show in every area of life. He was and is the star of our family. He was the best at everything. He was the one my father felt like should be his son." Darren's voice cracked. This was really hard on him to confess to me, and I didn't take it for granted. "When you mentioned the stuff about how you took a chance, hopped on an airplane, and all that stuff about changing, well, I did know that all too well."

My heart took over my head, and I reached over and placed my hand on top of his.

"Only I didn't leave the people who didn't believe in me behind." Was he giving me a dig because I left my hometown? "I stayed here to prove them wrong. I continued to work on my musical skills and started the local band. I might not have the best reputable bar in town, but I restored the lighthouse, I give my taxes, and I sure do take pride in being the Merry Maker with you, because honey, after you get a tickle in your fancy, I'm the one who will be left standing as the Merry Maker. Not you and me."

"Ha! I knew it! I knew you were the Merry Makers." Mae had jerked open the door. Her big pearly-white smile shined brighter than any mirror ball that would drop on New Year's Eve. "I was listening on the other side of the door."

"I never told you how Mae and I got our start." I pulled my hand off Darren's after I saw her looking at it. "She's a sneaky one."

"And, from what I hear, is really good at it." Darren stood up. "It appears as though we three will be working together to get this murder solved."

"And I'm going to use my investigative skills to get the story of a life-time." I was still searching for the big one that would hit the newswire, gaining me the biggest journalism awards to be had. Or at least a bigger job, since my sights were still to climb the ladder.

Holiday Junction was just a pit stop along the way.

"Uncork the bubbly," Mae muttered in an eerie voice for what were usually festive words. "Looks like you've got yourself a front-page story."

The countdown was on. And I wasn't referring to the new year.

CHAPTER ELEVEN

The supper the Stricklands hosted for Mae was very kind and didn't lack the hospitality I'd expected. Marge and Louise pulled out all the stops, from the fine china that'd been passed down from generation to generation to the family crest on the silverware to the monogrammed cloth napkins.

Millie Kay was in hog heaven.

"Did you see those napkins?" Mama gasped with delight. Mae and I had decided to ride back with her and Daddy in the golf cart.

Normally, I wouldn't ride with her, but the trolley had long since stopped for the night, and the chill in the air kept me from getting on the back of Darren's moped. And Mae needed a ride back, too, so I agreed to risk my life to ride with Mama.

The one good thing was she'd purchased one of those golf cart zip enclosures with a small heater, making the short ride back to her house bearable to the pacing heart and numbing fingers with which I'd gripped the side handlebar.

"Honey, did you happen to bring the cloth napkins?" Mama asked Daddy.

"No, dear. I just brought myself. I've told you that many times."

Daddy had hopped on an airplane a few months ago after realizing Mama wasn't going to come home.

The only things he even had in his suitcase were a toothbrush and some underwear. That was only because Mama had always made sure to tell us when we were going somewhere, "Do you have on clean underwear? Just in case you get in an accident and they have to take you to the hospital, you should have on clean underwear."

"I'm more than happy to run by your house and check on it as well as get some things to send to you." Mae was kind to offer.

"I always knew you were a nice young woman, even though Violet talked about you terrible." Mama might've had the best manners during social interaction, but behind the zip enclosure of this golf cart, she seemed to have lost her filter. "I can't tell you how many times I blessed you out."

In the distance, the white, gold, and silver lights strung all over Holiday Park twinkled. For a brief moment, my heart flipped. It looked like lightning bugs were having their own party to usher out the year. The moving lights were really the coming together of the wind whipping off the seaside and down the mountainside and meeting at the park. But for a second, it was fun to get lost in the idea that somewhere, there was just delight and not a murder hanging over the looming new year.

Though it was dark, I could feel Mae staring at me. She knew all too well what a bless out was, and it was not a "bless your heart." It was a telling off.

"Now dear." Daddy shifted, sending his gaze to the back of the golf cart to let me know he'd handle her. "I think Mae has a great idea to ship anything you want out here."

"We have to make a list," Mama agreed. She took a hard right at the stoplight and then another one on Heart Street. "Mae, do you think you'll be able to call your mama or even that handyman of yours and have him go get my napkins? I invited the Stricklands over for a New Year's Day lunch with all the good-luck fixings."

She brought the golf cart to a hard stop, jerking us forward. She'd yet to master the brake pedal, and my neck was starting to feel it.

"Mama!" I unzipped the plastic bubble around us. "You can't ask Mae to get something shipped to her right now. You'll just have to go see Leni McKenna."

"Really, it's no problem." Mae was just being kind to Mama and giving her what we called lip service.

She was making Mama think it was no problem to satisfy Mama, but in reality, Mae had no idea if Henry Bryant, the handyman at the campground Mae owned, would even want or be available to do it.

"Who's Lenni?" Mae asked and got out of the golf cart. Fortunately, we weren't harmed.

"She's a local woman who knits and crochets and is the town's tailor." Mama was quick to answer. "But I'd really like to have my own napkins so I can tell the Stricklands our family history."

Daddy had already jumped out to punch in the garage code so Mama could pull the golf cart in for the night.

"You better take a step back, or she'll run over your toes," I told Mae as the garage door started to open. I'd never seen a time when Mama had waited long enough for it to fully open until she drove in. Most of the time, she'd squeeze in before the door was fully open, and then she'd get out and punch the button to send the door back down.

"If you and Daddy are really going to live here forever, then there's no reason to hurry to get the napkins." What a silly thing for me to say because Mama skidded the golf cart to a halt, causing the most alarming tire screech before she bolted off the vehicle.

"You listen to me, young lady." Mama's mouth contorted, and the vein in her forehead popped out and started to pulse faster and faster as the anger built up inside of her.

"Uh-oh," was all Daddy had to say before he hightailed it into the house, leaving me there for the explosion that was going to erupt from Mama.

Her finger started to wag, her head started to bobble, and her eyes grew like a dragon's.

"I won't have you being unladylike and running all over the hours of the night with Darren Strickland. I will snatch you bald-headed if I catch you one more time letting him in that gate."

Her finger swung from me to the garage wall, where the side of the house closest to the gate was.

"Smart Southern women know their true value, and they don't give discounts." Mama moved her finger and jutted it at Mae. "Take Mae. Mary Elizabeth brought her up right, and look at that ring on her finger. Now she might've gotten off to a rough start, but take it from her."

"I, er, I..." Mae gave up trying to speak over Mama. She knew how a tongue-lashing went, and no matter how much she tried to raise her voice, Mama would match it and go an octave higher.

"If I don't start this courtship off the right way by hosting them the way we do it"—she meant Southern—"then you're gonna be playing second fiddle to your future in-laws, and I won't have it, Missy!"

My name wasn't Missy, but when she did call me that, it meant she was getting right with me, setting me straight, and there wasn't anything I could do.

"I'm gonna present you like the Southern belle you were taught to be and show off that you run that newspaper because you are a strong Southern woman." Mama would have liked to have made every word in that sentence "Southern," just to beat into my head that even though we weren't living in the South anymore, she was going to make sure we were representing.

"Yep. She's right." Mae rested her hands on her hips and gave hard nods with each one of Mama's words. I glared at her to let her know I was perturbed. "And I'll talk to her all about it tonight."

Mae grabbed my elbow.

"Right now too. While it's fresh in her mind." Mae swiftly jerked me out of the garage and around the house. "You need to listen to your mama, Violet Rhinehammer," she said in a loud tone over her shoulder, projecting her voice toward the garage.

"Have you lost your mind?" I jerked away from her. "You and I both know Darren Strickland and I don't have any sort of nightly rendezvous."

"Not yet. But maybe after I knock some sense into you after we figure out who murdered Hillary, you will." Mae flipped the squeaky latch on the gate door and swung it open.

"Whatever," I mumbled and spat on the silver metal piece.

"Really? That's not ladylike." Mae acted as though she'd been a debutante all her life when she was way worse as a child than I'd ever been, but I didn't remind her of her past.

"It's the only way to get it to stop squeaking for the time being." I moved the latch up and down, giving it a few more rounds of saliva so it didn't make noise. "Darren will be here to discuss—you know what? You're not supposed to know."

"The Merry Maker?" Mae nonchalantly asked in her normal voice as if it was known to the world.

"Shh!" I could see by the look in her eyes she darn well knew she wasn't supposed to mention that title.

Under her breath, she snickered her way back to the little garage I'd turned into my home. It wasn't any bigger than the travel trailer Mae lived in, but I found myself apologizing for the small space.

"It's adorable." She sloughed off her coat and hung it on one of the hooks next to the door. I had put those there to economize the space. "I love it."

While Mae took the opportunity to walk around the one room, which had many different distinctive areas, I told her what I'd done to the place.

"It was really an old garage that needed a good cleanup. The bones are great and sturdy. Plus it's got some nice insulation, though I did add some extra," I told her as she ran-walked into the small yet functional kitchen.

I didn't have to tell Mae how hard it was to redo a structure since that was what she'd done with a lot of the rentable campers she offered to guests.

"I didn't want the feel of a redone garage. I wanted it to look like a home. Vern McKenna had a set of old French doors at his shed. He gave those to me, so I swapped out the original single door for those." I was really proud of my handiwork. It was something I'd never done before, and I had to say that moving to a place where I didn't know anyone or rely on anyone to help me really did boost my confidence in all areas of my life.

"On the outside, I opted to pay a little more for a metal roof because with the weather elements like the sea air and the soggy mountain terrain, I knew the shingles would have to be cleaned frequently, and in the long run, it would've been more costly." I found myself surprised at the words I was using.

Since when did I ever live on a budget?

"In the daylight, you'll be able to see where I painted the outside a fresh coat of glossy gray-green paint." It was a great neutral color that fit the town and any decorations I was going to use for each holiday.

"I love this kitchen." Mae ran her hand down the countertop I'd made out of plywood and covered in several coats of high-gloss varnish. "I'd kill to have a full stove."

That was one of the pricey items I did purchase for the L-shaped space because it was one of those one-piece stove and hood sets.

"I bought the cabinets straight from the local home improvement store." It was really just one of those big-box chain stores.

"I love it. I really do." Mae beamed at me, and I watched as she opened the refrigerator I'd kept stocked with fruits, water, and alcohol. "Let me see the bedroom."

We walked around the small wall I'd erected to separate the kitchen and headed past the folding solid-wood room divider where I had put my bedroom. It was the farthest area away from the front door.

The bed took up most of the space, but the mattress was quality.

Mae sat on the bed and bounced a couple of times.

"Comfy," she gushed and flung herself back on it, resting her hands on her belly. "I'd kill for a real bed."

"It's important for sleep and stress," I told her and walked over to the two reclaimed swinging doors that provided access to the garage loft. "This is really cool."

Mae sat up and watched as I pulled down the attic-access ladder I'd had installed so I could utilize the loft.

Mae jumped up and headed straight up the ladder to the loft area, which was really only enough room for one person.

"Oh my goodness." She stood at the top rung and held on to the rails, looking down at me. "This is a dream. Do I get to sleep here?"

"That was why I created it." I was so pleased she liked it.

I didn't tell her, but after she'd called to tell me she was coming for a visit and needed to get away, I'd taken the space I initially planned to use for storage and turned it into a little sleep area with a mattress on the floor, a few larger beanbag chairs, and a couple of stand-up lights for when I did have guests.

That was more than likely going to be rare now. The area still turned out really cute.

"The bed alone is delicious!" She'd already disappeared up there. Her voice floated down the ladder.

I waited to see if she was going to come down. Then, after a couple of minutes, I climbed the ladder.

"You don't have to sleep up here if you don't want to," I said. "Mae, are you okay?"

"Mm-hmm," she sleepily said and rolled over on her side, facing me. She curled her legs up into a ball. Her eyes were closed. The soft sound of her heavy breathing led into an even fainter snore.

Smiling, I shook my head and descended back down the ladder. I closed the sliding doors behind me.

The French doors opened, and I grabbed the only thing on my nightstand—a hardcover cozy mystery novel—so I could throw it at whoever let themselves in my home.

"I've got a weapon," I called out and peeked around the room divider with the book held over my head.

"A book?" Darren stood at the door with his hoodie over his head. "I need to get you a bat or something."

"You could've knocked." I set the book down on the couch once I made it over there.

"I didn't want Millie Kay to hear." He was right.

"You could've called or texted." I walked off to the kitchen. "Do you want a drink?"

"Sure. I'll take a beer," he said. I heard the air go out of the cushion on the couch, so I didn't need to tell him to make himself at home.

I opened the refrigerator and grabbed him and myself a beer.

When I returned to the space I considered the living area, family-room style, I noticed he was reading my book.

"You make fun of it, but it does help me think of ways for us to find out who might've had motive to kill Hillary." I handed him the beer.

"I think you are spending too much time reading these things." He sat it back down where he found it and took a swig of the beer. "Where's Mae?"

"Some help she's going to be tonight. She climbed up to the little loft and fell fast asleep as soon as her head hit the mattress." To be a little selfish, I was kind of glad she was asleep because now I felt like I could have some alone time with Darren since our recent turn of events.

"Then we should probably get going." By the way he stood up with his coat still on, I could sense he was talking about the Merry Maker job instead of the kiss and conversation we'd had earlier.

"Sure. Let me get my coat back on." I handed him my beer and went to get my coat off the hook.

"I'll help you." He'd set the beers on the small end table by the couch. He took my coat from me and helped manipulate each arm into the correct hole before he turned me around and zipped me up. "We can't have you getting sick before the Sparkle Ball."

There was something lazily seductive in the way he looked at me. I quickly turned away.

"There won't be a ball if we don't find the killer." I picked up my bottle and took a big swig to help swallow the lump in my throat.

"Speaking of the killer." He opened the door. I noticed he'd not taken any more drinks of his beer before we headed out the door. "I've been thinking about that."

Without saying it, both of us made sure we stayed hidden in the shadows of the moon. Mama had made it very clear at supper that she knew he was coming and going, only she wasn't connecting the Merry Maker issue. She was well aware Darren and I were co-Merry Makers, but luckily, she knew how important it was to keep the secret, so in her own little weird way, she wanted to believe we were sneaking around in a relationship.

She was wrong, at least for now.

Once we made it safely down the sidewalk and off of Heart Street, we were free to talk openly.

Holiday Junction was a ghost town after dark when a festival wasn't going on. Though we were in the full swing of the New Year's activities, I had to believe it was the knowledge that Hillary's killer was still out there that kept people from moving about during the nighttime.

Good for us. It only helped us escape the rumors involved in being seen together.

"Fern Banks owes me a favor." The sound of her name coming out of his mouth made my skin crawl.

Or maybe it was the goose bumps from the frosty cold air, but either way, it was uncomfortable.

"I called her," he said and then I knew it was her that made my skin crawl. "I told her I needed her to work at the bar in the morning because you and I are going to run all over town to get some motives now that my dad has given us the go-ahead."

"What did she say?" I should've focused on his saying we were going to start our little investigation, but I had to think of her.

"She was fine with it." He kept his hands in the pocket of his jacket and picked up the pace as we hoofed it down the sidewalk past Holiday Park. "I am also going to take the opportunity when I see her to ask her about what she mentioned about Hillary while she was passed out."

"Don't you think it was just innocent because Fern saw Hillary protesting?" I asked, probing more into what he was thinking.

"There's something you don't know," he said. He barely made it past the Merry Maker figure that would be dropped at midnight to signal the new year when Mayor Paisley joined us. "Hillary threw rotten tomatoes at Fern when Fern was crowned the high school prom queen."

We both bent down and patted Mayor Paisley.

My eyes grew, and the sound of footsteps was fast approaching. I knew they had to belong to Kristine Whitlock, Mayor Paisley's owner.

"And?" I hurried him to tell me before Kristine made it to us.

"She made it a life mission to always tell Hillary she'd get the last laugh every time she saw Hillary. The other night, when I took her back to the lighthouse, her words had shifted from the normal." His words had a bite. "She said someone should get rid of Hillary. Called her the village nuisance."

The goose bumps were long gone.

Now I had the willies.

CHAPTER TWELVE

"What are you two doing out here this late?" Kristine's smile lines deepened, as did the wrinkles on her forehead. Strands of her long salt-and-pepper hair peeked out of the knit hat covering the top of her head.

"We are, um…" I wanted to use my normal tactic of reversing someone's question so I could avoid it altogether. Mayor Paisley's current potty break didn't give me that option. "Working."

"Working?" She shifted her eyes between Darren and me before they grew as big as the full moon hanging overhead. "Are you the Merry Maker?"

"Now why on earth would you think that?" Darren nervously laughed. "No, heck no."

"Yeah. No." The word came out in a Southern extended vowel sound, making the single word syllable more like three. "That's ridiculous, but if you see the Merry Maker, please let me know so I can do a story on him. *Ahem*." I cleared my throat. "Or her."

Kristine's eyes held a glint of wonder, the kind that meant she was trying to feel out the situation. The one that told me she was too smart to fall for the excuse that Darren and I were working. Why on earth would Darren and I be working together?

"Chief Strickland." My hands flew in the air before my fingers landed on a piece of my long hair and twisted it around. "The murder," I sputtered. "Hillary. The killer."

My mind lost all sense. I couldn't help but think about Hillary being upset that a dog was named mayor. Ridiculous of me to think Kristine or even Hubert had anything to do with Hillary's murder.

Right?

"What Violet is trying to spit out is a big secret, really." Darren's jaw set. His head twisted around as he looked before he slightly bent in toward Kristine's personal space and whispered, "This is on the down-low, but I think you could be of help."

"What?" The wrinkle lines on Kristine's face softened.

"He's at a standstill about the murder of Hillary Stevens and has asked us to look into it. Me because Hillary and I were friends back in the day and Violet because she's already helped out a few times."

"She does have that keen nose like a dog." Kristine nodded and quickly followed up. "Not meaning you're a dog but that you can sniff out things normal humans can't. Like solutions to crimes. You know."

"Yes. I do have that keen sense of smell." I tapped my nose, just trying to get the conversation over with as quickly as possible. "That's why this is all hush. Not even Millie Kay knows."

"But you mentioned I might be able to help. How so?" she asked and picked up the black-and-white Boston terrier who was actually voted on as mayor.

"You're friends with most people in the town, and you are at all the events, including the town council event for the mini-village." My words landed hard on her as her face grew tense.

"I know you hear things, and well, any sort of information will be helpful." Darren pointed back at the Holiday Park Fountain, where the Merry Maker New Year's Eve drop would happen. "Holiday Junction certainly doesn't want to start the year off on a wrong foot."

"No. I suppose not." The condensation from her heavy sigh rolled up and danced around her eyes. "I did hear someone arguing with her."

"Let me guess. Fern Banks."

"You know Fern. She puts her foot in her mouth all the time, and she's at every event, representing the titles she holds." Kristine was trying to make a good argument for Fern, since she held all the titles in the beauty queen department.

Fern was one of those serial beauty queen contestants who was trying to win every title so she could make it to the Miss USA pageant. Those crowns also meant she had to go to all the events, like the mayor.

Only the mayor was nicer.

I stopped myself from saying that out loud. Everyone loved Fern. Everyone but me.

"I'm not saying she did anything. You guessing who I've been thinking about means you've heard it from others." This was the bit Kristine would hang on to if it got out that she told us or anyone else about Fern's behavior toward Hillary and Kristine confronted Fern.

"We would never tell anyone anything you said unless we found out this did have to do with Hillary's death and Fern was arrested for the murder." Darren put her at ease. "Can you give us any other examples or situations where you've seen Hillary as a member of the village council?"

"Good question," I told Darren.

"Honestly, Hillary would show up at every meeting, and most months we had nothing to talk about. But when we have the slightest change in the village, like the amendment to use LED bulbs on the Christmas tree at Holiday Park or even when…" She paused. Her brows drew together, and her lips twitched as she looked at me. "Violet took over the *Junction Journal* and moved it to the cottage. Hillary was beside herself, saying the cottage didn't need to be updated or modernized, and the clapboards were dingy and rotted to show the true beauty and age."

I couldn't stop my face from doing the thing. My nose curled, making my lips pucker. My jaw tensed, causing my eyes to cloud with images of the village official who came to make sure a permit had been pulled to do the work. It was a hassle.

"She's the one who made me go through all those hoops?" I asked after we had to make sure the cottage couldn't be listed on the historical register.

"I never wanted you to find out because it all worked out for you. Not Hillary so much," she muttered. "But that's all I know. I guess you can ask other Village Council members."

"When is the next meeting?" I asked.

"Oh." She shook her head. "Not until the new year." She rubbed down Paisley's back. "She's shivering, so we need to get home and get back in bed. This is what happens when guests feed her too many treats."

"Can I ask you one more question?" I was dying to come out with it. "I understand Hillary wasn't fond of a dog being the mayor either."

"Of course she wasn't. But it was already a long-standing tradition well before Paisley was voted in." Kristine rolled her eyes. "As we all know, it's only to help raise money for the tourism since the Village Council resides as the government. She was mad because we told her a cat couldn't run."

"A cat?" I'd not heard this little fact.

"Yes. She has, had—heck, I don't even know if it's still living—but when Paisley ran her first term, Hillary had entered a cat into the race." Kristine shook her head. "What if someone is allergic to cats? Or even better, gets scratched by a cat during a photo opportunity?"

"I guess people could be allergic to dogs." I shrugged and threw it out there.

"Regardless, she was shot down and got mad at all the owners who had candidates for mayor." Kristine tsked. "I've got to go."

"Thanks, Kristine." Darren waved goodbye while I just stood there.

There was silence between Darren and me as we crept back along the path down to the seaside. The lighthouse's light twirled from the top and drifted along the sea before it shone on the banks and then us as it began the journey back to the ocean.

"That's a real historical building." I gestured to his home. "Not a cottage. What is it with Hillary?"

"Was it," Darren corrected me. "I'm sorry. I know her, and she really didn't like change. At some point, her radical ideas got out of hand, and let's say when I bought the lighthouse years ago, she stopped talking to me. She felt it should've stayed in the hands of the village, but it was going to be so costly to fix it up that it suddenly didn't seem so important to the tourism."

"I guess I can't hold all the issues she gave me with the cottage against her because she's dead, but I can say how I felt. At that time, I scoured and probed for who could've been giving me a hard time and no one said a word. I almost wrote a letter to the paper, but I needed my job, and I didn't know if I was going to step on toes." I snapped my fingers. "She totally stepped on someone's toes. They'd had enough."

"We certainly know she and Fern had a fight in public, which will let me talk to Fern tomorrow." He picked up the pace on our way back toward the neighborhood we had to cut through to get to the woods that would lead us to Vern's shed.

The temperature had turned almost bitter, and the wind whipping up around us didn't make it any better.

"We also have Berta Bristol." I started to rattle off all the names associated with Hillary over the last couple of days. "Denise Kenner and Troy Kenner."

"That's four." Inside his pocket, Darren's hands pulled closer together, making his shoulders slump to keep away the cold. "I can't imagine one of them physically placing Hillary in that position because none of them are strong enough."

"Troy is," I confirmed. "We need to get all four of their alibis."

"I'm sure my dad has done that," Darren stated the obvious.

"I mean get them talking, and then they might say something that would place them near the scene because you can't move a body like that without someone noticing," I said as we took our first steps into the spooky woods.

The moon still hung high in the night sky with the blanket of twinkling stars. It was like the universe was having its own little New Year's celebration. It was a beautiful sight, and if I weren't freezing and ready to call it a day, I'd have taken the time to sit and watch from the window of my cute little garage home.

"I still can't get over that people around here voted a dog in as mayor." I had to break the eerie silence surrounding us. "I mean, she's adorable and all."

"It's for charity." Darren didn't tell me anything I already didn't know. The branches snapped under his feet with each step.

"Yeah. I know. And it's a good tourist attraction," I said because when I first came to Holiday Junction, I'd lived at the Jubilee Inn, where Mayor Paisley lived with Kristine and Hubert Whitlock, the inn's owners. And I also knew the town was actually a village and the council had the power of mayoral duties like other towns across the United States.

When they decided to make the mayor an animal, it cost one dollar a vote, and the money went back into tourism for Holiday Junction. The only duties Mayor Paisley had to attend were ribbon-cutting ceremonies and a few photo ops here and there. People lined up for hours to get their photo with Mayor Paisley, and donations were taken at those events.

It turned out to be a great marketing tool for Holiday Junction.

One thing that wasn't great for tourism was a dead body.

My mind circled back to the task at hand when I saw the faint light glowing from the window of Vern's secret shed.

"Where do you think we need to put the Merry Maker sign?" I asked Darren. He'd pulled a note off the shed door and used his phone's flashlight to read it.

"Vern got tired of waiting for us." He handed me the note. "He says it's inside."

"Where are we putting the sign?" I asked again so we could stick it in the ground and go home.

"Like I said, Cup of Cheer." He'd told me that earlier when I'd asked, but I was hoping he'd changed his mind.

"We had a Merry Maker event on the beach near the lighthouse already." I wasn't sold on the idea.

He opened the door, and the warmth of the interior hit my face. The smell of ashes from the potbelly wood stove in the corner of the shed told of the fire Vern had set that day, but it was long gone, even though the heat was still inside.

"You need to make a good write-up about it. The symbolism of the sea going in and out with the prospect of new possibilities."

Dang. Darren had a great idea.

CHAPTER THIRTEEN

"Where did you put it?" Mae walked around the room divider, her curly honey-blond hair sticking out all over the place.

"Put what?" I asked, looking back with my laptop in one hand and a cup of coffee in the other.

When Darren and I finally placed the wood structure that looked like a mirror ball in front of Cup of Cheer, it was too late to go to the office to write up today's New Year's festivities.

The very idea of someone seeing us made my nerves so electric and hyped up that when I got home, I should've fallen in my bed from mental exhaustion, but I was wide-awake.

Instead of forcing myself to lie there and think about the schedule of events Louise had asked me to post, I got up and logged in from home, where I was able to write up a quick time, place, and event.

"Hold on," I said to Mae. "Grab yourself a cup of coffee, and I'll finish writing this up."

Not that I didn't do my job last night. I just didn't give the normal detailed description the readers of the *Junction Journal* were accustomed to.

"No harm, no foul," I said as I finished typing up all the events' descriptions in detail so when someone did click on the *Journal*'s list of holiday events, they'd be able to see what each one was about.

I sighed, shut the laptop, and placed it on the side table as I curled my legs up underneath me so I could give Mae all my attention.

"So?" She eased down on the couch with her full cup of coffee.

"I think we should definitely go to Resting Grinch Face." I put the cup up to my lips and took a sip. "Oh, yeah. I forgot you had no idea what that was. I've not seen it, either, but I hear it's a really great time." I put my free hand on my chest. "It's an event with improv, stand-up, and sketch comedy, paired with huge prize money. Kinda like the mini-village."

"I'm talking about the Merry Maker." Mae wasn't going to drop it.

"I'd rather not talk about it. The less I talk or think about it, the less of a chance the secret will get out." I got up and walked over to the coffeepot.

"Who on earth will I tell?" Mae sounded a little put off. "Fine."

I guessed my silence had told her to move on to a different topic.

"Or were you and Darren sneaking out for a midnight stroll?" Dang, she wasn't going to let it go. "I think we can talk about it. I flew out all this way to spend time with you, unlike the way I'd spend most of my time when you lived in Normal—getting away from you."

I nearly spat my coffee out of my mouth.

"I knew it. But hearing you admit it really cracks me up." I should've been offended by what she'd said, but I wasn't. I knew I wanted the scoop from her, and I was going to do everything my little journalist body could do to get the story. "If following you around and hunting you down was going to get the inside information for my show or even the *Gazette*, I was willing to be a thorn in your side."

"I'm glad I'm here." She smiled and looked down into her coffee. "Honestly, Ellis is so hard to have a relationship with. I'm not sure how to navigate her. She moved into the campground with Ty, of course. She complains about everything from the water pressure to the darkness at night."

"Doesn't she know she's living in a camper on a campground?" I pointed out the obvious.

"Oh, yeah. I almost blew my top when she complained about the moon being too bright." Mae snorted. "Then she wanted us to get some lights to light the way around the lake, but I told her it was a campground, not a neighborhood. It was a place where people literally vacationed. They didn't really live there. They come to Happy Trails Campground to look at the moon, stars, nature, and landscape in and around the Daniel Boone National Forest."

"I'm sorry." I frowned. "I know Ellis can be difficult, and I have no idea how to help you, but the fact she not only got engaged but married before you is something, um…" I searched to find the right word.

"So Ellis?" Mae said more than asked.

"Yeah." I could tell by Mae's body language she already had her pulse on her soon-to-be sister-in-law and Ellis's love for the limelight. "I'm more than happy for her to take the spotlight." She looked up at me. "Honestly, I'm glad she's taken away all of Mother's attention from me because that woman and I just don't see eye to eye."

Mae sat up a little straighter.

"What about you? Can you tell me anything about Darren?" Mae offered a gentle smile, the kind that told me she was really listening and cared.

"He was nowhere on my radar." I put both hands around the mug, leaning my hip on the edge of the counter.

"Until?" Mae fished for more.

"Until we went up into his lighthouse and sat on the top with our legs dangling over." The memory was seared into my heart like a cow brand. "That was our first moment."

"By 'moment,' you mean 'kiss'?" Mae's tone did that uptick thingy that meant she wanted more information.

"Don't get so excited." Even though I thought the conversation would go in a different direction after that, it didn't. "We stalled after that, and recently, we had another one."

I didn't tell her the intensity of the most recent one because it was still something I was enjoying, and last night, he'd stayed so far away from me that it made me think I had some sort of contagious illness.

"And?" Mae dragged one leg up under her and leaned a little closer. "Last night?"

My lips formed a flat line with a hint of a smile.

"Not a thing. All business." I set the mug in the sink. "I have to go get ready for work."

"Wait." She stopped me and twisted around, looking over the back of the couch at me as I walked across the room toward the bathroom. "What about Hillary Stevens? And the Merry Maker?"

"After I work a little at the office this morning, I'm going to check on a few leads. One of them being Troy Kenner." I stopped at the bathroom door. "I want you to go explore and see if you can find the Merry Maker's sign."

"I get it. You don't want me hanging around while you work." She stood up and walked into the kitchen area. "But you can't get rid of me while you snoop around for the killer."

Over the next thirty minutes, I got ready for the day and started walking to the main street, where most of the shops and stores were located. Brewing Beans was always my first stop.

"You're a little late." Hazelynn Hudson, the owner, pointed at the shelf where they put the call-ahead orders, only I didn't have to call ahead.

Every day, she knew I'd be in, and every day, she had my usual drink ready.

"Bring it over to me and I'll get you a fresh one." After I picked up the to-go cup, she waved me over. "What's going on? You're never late."

"I guess I was just so tired I needed a little extra sleep." I handed the cup to her and tried to lie the best I could, but Hazelynn had gotten to know me a little too well after we'd put our heads together during the Halloweenie kerfuffle.

"You are looking into Hillary Stevens, aren't you?" she asked and took the lid off the cup so she could dump the contents into the sink behind the bar.

I nodded, knowing I could use her to my advantage.

"If you have any tips, I'd love to know how to get in front of Denise Kenner and her son Troy." Holiday Junction was a tiny village, and it was no joke to say that everyone who lived here knew one another. "Anything to help is appreciated."

"Denise loves our holiday crème brûlée coffee. Every year around this time, she comes in and buys it by the to-go box. Troy makes sure she gets a box the first day it's available." Hazelynn was telling me to bribe Denise. "Would you like to add a box of holiday crème brûlée coffee to your order?" she asked and poured me a fresh cup of the regular house morning blend. "It'll only take me a second to brew a fresh pot."

"You know, I would." I liked how she thought. She sat my cup on the counter and walked off to get the box of coffee.

"And I'll put it on the *Junction Journal*'s tab." She was a sly one.

"You do that." I agreed because when I glanced up at the price board behind the counter, the price of a box of coffee was a lot higher than I'd anticipated. "How long have you known Hillary?"

Now seemed like a great time to start asking people in the community about Hillary Stevens and getting a real profile of who she really was or—at least how the public saw her.

"Her whole life, she's been a little troublemaker. I'm not saying it negatively, but she was always into something that wasn't good," Hazelynn said. She continued to talk to me as she took different ingredients and sprinkled them into the coffee beans she'd already put into the grinder. "She was a little more pious than the other children. When they added Darren's store"—she referred to the jiggle joint—"to the mini-village, Hillary stole the mini beer cans in the display. That's when Chief Strickland took a real vested interest because Hillary's little act had to do with someone he loved."

"What did he do?" I asked above the whirl of the grinder.

"He raided her home and found all the mini cans hidden under her mattress all smashed." Hazelynn hit the off button.

"When did you last see her?" I wondered.

"Early the morning of her death." Hazelynn pointed at the door. "She was peeping inside. I knew it was time for the ribbon-cutting ceremony and the mini-village display to open, and it was like her to cause problems. I called Chief Strickland."

"You called him?" This was the first time I was hearing this.

"Mm-hmm." Hazelynn had put the freshly ground coffee grinds in the industrial coffee maker and hit the on button. She walked back over to the counter and stood there with her arms crossed. "He asked me if she was doing anything illegal, and I told him no." She snorted a sarcastic laugh. "He said to call dispatch if there was a real reason for them to come out."

"Really?" I asked.

"Yep." She sucked in a deep breath. Her eyes grazed my shoulder. I looked behind me at the long line that'd formed since I'd been there. "Not his family, so not important."

"Wow. That's crazy." I wanted to stick that in my notes about things I'd found out while I snooped around today. "Maybe with the coffee, I can score what Denise Kenner will believe is an interview."

"This is her kryptonite." Hazelynn was confident about it, and I was going to trust her.

"I'll go sit over here." I pointed at the open table closest to the window, where I sat down and pulled out my phone. I jumped on the *Junction Journal*'s website and made a post about the hot topic that would soon be floating around Holiday Junction while I waited for the box of coffee.

The New Year is almost here, and the Merry Maker has posted the last hurrah of the year for Holiday Junction. I do not believe this particular spot for celebration could have been chosen for any other reason than paying tribute to Hillary Stevens, the village resident who loved all things about the Merry Maker. It appears that we will be toasting the New Year with tea at Cup of Cheer located on Holiday Junction's seaside.

I can't think of a better way to pay tribute to one of Holiday Junction's most loyal citizens, who not only lived for everything the village stood for but for what the village's founding fathers envisioned for Holiday Junction.

"You look happier than before." Hazelynn brought me the cardboard container and a few stacked cups.

"I found out the Merry Maker has picked the New Year's celebration spot." I stood up and put my phone in my coat pocket. "Or did you already know?" I gave Hazelynn the side-eye as if she already knew, making it appear that I was accusing her of being the Merry Maker.

"Are you joking? I barely have time to brew my own beans these days. Where is the sign?" she asked.

"Cup of Cheer." I could see she was taken aback, making me wonder if I'd let Darren pick the wrong place. "I can't help but think the Merry Maker knew Hillary and her love for this town, so ushering out the year with her family's place does seem like a good idea. At least her family might have some comfort."

Now I was really regretting agreeing with Darren.

"I think it's a perfect place." She took the liberty to push the chair back up to the table before I could do it. "I have no idea how the Merry Maker does it. Always picks the best spot."

"If you ever get a hint of who it is, I'd love to know that too." For good measure, I had to throw that in there. "I like to get all the good scoops first."

"I know you do. So good luck. I really hope you can get some information from Denise." Hazelynn started to walk away.

"Hazelynn," I called her back. "Is there a list of founding fathers anywhere?"

"Yes. In the Welcome Center. There's a bronze plaque next to the door." She smiled. "If you didn't know it was there, you'd miss it. It's small with only four names. Bristol, Steinner, Kenner, and Stevens."

"As in Berta Bristol, Denise Kenner, Hillary Stevens?" I asked, knowing that two of these people were on my short list of suspects. "Steinner?" I'd heard the name but with my current lack of caffeine wasn't able to place it.

"Gail. Schoolteacher at the elementary." She recalled my memory.

"The teacher who had the Rapunzel display." I snapped my fingers before I picked up the coffee box. My day just got a little longer. "School isn't in session, is it?"

"No. They are still off for break, and if you were married with children, you'd know that." Hazelynn's interest in my marital status caught me off guard. "But that's none of my business."

"I see you've been spending too much time with Millie Kay." I shook a finger. "Just get any and all nonsense about me getting hitched out of your head. Besides"—I shrugged my right shoulder—"you gotta find a partner before I can do that."

"I hear Darren Strickland is available," she trilled.

My brows jumped up on my forehead.

"There might be some rumblings about you two spending a lot of time together." If she only knew it was because of the Merry Maker. "And they weren't from Millie Kay."

"We've been on a few dates. That's all." I lifted my hand in the air and wiggled it. "No ring on this finger. Speaking of rings…" I smiled. "I don't want to ring in the new year before we get this killer behind bars."

CHAPTER FOURTEEN

I'd made it out of Brewing Beans just in time to grab the trolley. Otherwise, I would have run the risk of getting semihot coffee to Denise Kenner, and I needed all the ammunition possible so I could get in front of her.

"Ceramic Celebration, huh?" Goldie Bennett wore a headband that had mirror balls on springs. Her slightest move made them wiggle, giving me a little enjoyment. "I took little Lizzy there a few weeks ago. She wanted to make her mom a jewelry box for her birthday."

"I bet that took a while." I'd never done any sort of ceramics, but the project sounded like a big one.

"Heck no. Lizzy just slapped some paint on the already-made mold. The shop glazed it after she was done, and we picked it up in time for her mom's birthday celebration." Goldie slammed the brakes of the trolley on, flinging a few passengers forward, who desperately scrambled to get their footing.

The trolley door slid open right in front of the Strickland compound.

Darren got on and looked around. Our eyes caught. Without him looking, he took change from his pocket and shoved it in the fare box.

The *clink* of the coins hitting the steel bottom resounded.

When it was apparent he was taking the open seat next to me, I scooted over more than I needed to and looked up at the large rearview mirror Goldie used to see inside of the trolley.

There was a glint of wonder and amusement in her eyes when she glanced at me before pulling the lever for the trolley door to close.

"Where are you going, Darren?" she asked him, since he'd not announced his destination when he got in.

"Wherever Violet is going." He nudged me. Goldie grinned. "Ceramic Celebration it is."

"You were headed to see Denise without me." His voice held a smug tone. "I was just catching a ride to the journal cottage because I saw the article you wrote about the Merry Maker."

"I was on my way to the office." I pointed at the container of coffee on the floor between my feet. "Hazelynn sidetracked me. Told me how much Denise loved her holiday crème brûlée blend, and I couldn't let anyone go without their daily dose of caffeine."

"And you didn't think to call or text me?" he asked.

"What were you doing at your parents' house? Were you talking to your dad without me?" I asked.

"I went by to grab a couple of biscuits." He opened the small paper sack in his grip. "It'll go well with coffee and ceramics."

"You know, I made my mama a clay-looking bowl once when I was in elementary school," I told Goldie since her silence after Darren got on had made it clear she was listening for any romance gossip.

"Yeah, I made a few of those myself." Darren wasn't privy to Goldie's eavesdropping.

"Ceramic Celebration isn't anything like that unless you're a serious artist. Mostly, they have those premade concrete pieces you get to paint, and they kiln it to the glaze you want. That type of thing. Lizzy put so much paint on the jewelry box, I bet Denise had to scrape some off." Goldie laughed and moved her conversation on to what she and her husband, Elvin, were doing for New Year's. "We decided we'd babysit the grands. Joey and Chance will be easy to get down. Not little Lizzy. She's a smart one. We turned the clock back at nine o'clock last year on everything but the microwave and told them it was midnight because they'd worn Elvin and me out. We weren't going to make it to midnight."

She snickered and swung the wheels of the trolley to a hard right going down toward the seaside.

"We made a big to-do out of it. We snapped the poppers and blew the horns, even yelling, 'Happy New Year.' But wouldn't you know Lizzy pointed at the microwave and said it was only nine o'clock." Goldie tsked. "Elvin and I gave up. They were wired at midnight."

"Stop the trolley!" I screamed, jumped up, and grabbed the box of coffee. "Stop!" I curled my arm around the bar for stability.

"This isn't Ceramic Celebration." Goldie brought the trolley to a screeching halt.

"I know but I need off." I turned back at Darren just as she opened the door. "Come on." I jerked with my head.

"What on earth is wrong with you?" he asked once we were off the trolley and Goldie was well on her way with the rest of the passengers.

"I just saw Hillary Stevens." I took off in the direction of the girl I'd seen who'd run into Louise.

"I think you need to drink that coffee because she's dead." He stopped jogging with me toward the girl in the hooded sweatshirt.

"That's the girl who ran into your mother!" I yelled behind me. The coffee sloshed inside the box. "She said it was Hillary!"

The girl gave a slight glance over her shoulder and picked up her speed. She took a sharp turn and dashed toward the ocean.

"Hey! Stop!" I yelled. My jog became a full run. "Stop! People think you're dead!"

The rush of waves crashing against the shore and the sound of our footsteps pounded against the sand. The wind and falling snowflakes whipped in my hair as the sand shifted beneath my feet, and I got closer to Hillary.

The sense of urgency made my heart race. The saltwater spray hit harder the closer we got to the shoreline.

My chest heaved up and down with the exhilarating feeling of catching up to her once she realized there was no farther to go unless she dove into the ocean.

Out of nowhere, Darren bolted past me and it didn't take long before he caught up with Hillary. He literally had to leap into the air, take her down, and tug her hoodie off her head.

"Troy?" Darren's face contorted into confusion. The waves rolled along the sandy beach, only inches from hitting his body.

"Troy Kenner?" I asked when I realized his long hair made Louise and everyone else think he was Hillary.

CHAPTER FIFTEEN

"**W**hy did you take off?" Darren had hoisted Troy up to his feet.

"I'm not here to create any trouble, Darren. You know I don't like conflict." He spoke to Darren but looked at me. "I don't have any comment."

"You think I'm here for an interview?" I asked him.

"Yeah. Why else would be you yelling for me? I've heard about you." He glared at me. His gloved hands were curled into fists. "So I'm going to be on my way now."

"Troy, we just want to talk about Hillary." Darren's voice was gentle. Almost mesmerizing. "We are trying to figure out who'd do this to her."

Troy shoved his hands back into the pockets of his hoodie. His eye zeroed in on the box of coffee.

"I know, man. I haven't spent a lot of time with you and her over the past years, but I still care." Darren seemed to be confessing to something I didn't know about, but I was here to listen and ask later. "All we want to know is if you knew anything."

Troy shivered.

"Would you like a cup of coffee?" I offered since I had the stack of to-go cups and the coffee.

"Yeah. Sure." He threw a chin, and when I held out the cups, he took the one on top. He used both hands to steady the cup while I filled it up.

"Darren?" I offered him a cup.

"No. I'm good." He was laser focused on Troy and started to batter him with questions. "What was Hillary up to recently?"

"She had this strange theory the Merry Maker wasn't from around here. Something about how the places were too obvious, almost like the Merry Maker didn't know the ins and outs of Holiday Junction." His account of what Hillary had been up to didn't sit too well with me.

Darren shifted his weight. A sure sign he was as uncomfortable with the subject as I was.

"She thought for sure the Merry Maker was going to host the New Year's final celebration at the mini-village at the Welcome Center." He sipped on the coffee between his sentences about Hillary's final hours. "She was sure the Merry Maker came from the woods because she said she followed the sandy trail of the Merry Maker during Halloweenie but lost the trail over Thanksgiving."

"You think the Merry Maker killed her?" I asked, trying to get around the fact that I had dragged the Merry Maker sign from the woods to Darren's lighthouse that night.

"If she was right, the Merry Maker would do anything to keep his identity secret." Troy didn't look at me or at Darren as if he suspected that we were the Merry Maker.

"Maybe the Merry Maker was at the Welcome Center and she confronted him." His words began to run together as my head swirled with ideas of how to convince him that the Merry Maker was not a suspect.

"No." I shook my head. "According to the autopsy report, Hilary was murdered somewhere else. Her body was placed in the mini-village."

"Placed?" The look on his face wasn't a killer's. He truly had not known the particulars of how Hillary was found.

It told me he didn't kill her but still left me with questions I'd love to have answered.

"Merry Maker," he grumbled with a tone of revenge. A coldness contracted along the muscles in my back, leaving a trail of goose bumps.

He was on a mission to uncover the Merry Maker's identity, and I had to do something about it.

"I really don't think it was the Merry Maker," I blurted out. "I don't know who the Merry Maker is, but I do know I get a lot of incoming emails from an untraceable server." I nervously laughed. "Trust me. I looked because I'd love to score an interview with him. Or her." I shrugged.

"I think it's him." Troy slowly nodded.

"Either way, I had been emailing back and forth with the Merry Maker during the time Curtis placed Hillary's time of death." Troy gave me a questioning stare. "I had to get the inside scoop on where the Merry Maker was going to host the last hurrah of the year, what spot so I could get it into the online paper before it went into the printed paper." I grabbed for my phone and started to bring up the online paper. "See. I got the online article up. And I couldn't do that without the Merry Maker."

Troy leaned in a little and looked at the phone. His eyes dragged up to meet mine.

I shrugged. He rocked back on the heels of his shoes.

"Why are you accusing me of killing her?" Troy tossed the question to Darren. "You knew I had sacrificed a future for myself to stay put in this nutjob town."

"I didn't accuse you. I followed Violet here, and when she told me it was Hillary, I knew it wasn't, but you wouldn't stop." Darren gestured to Troy's hair. "I haven't seen you in a while, and your hair is so long, I think my mom really did think you were Hillary the morning you ran into her."

"Which makes me question where you were going." This was only one of the questions.

"My mom and I had a fight. I stormed out of the shop and took off." He sucked his cheeks in and then shook his head and said, "Hillary had come in that morning before the shop opened. She said she'd tried to stop and get a coffee at Brewing Beans but they were closed. She mentioned Hazelynn told her to stop peeping and that she was going to call the cops. Hillary took off and came to the shop. Now that I'm set to take over after Mom retires, I'm there all the time. I let Hillary in because she knew it was going to be the day the mini-village's new additions would be judged, and it was a busy time for the shop."

The faint crunching sound as the snow started to fall and blow across the sand mixed with a howling of the gusty wind and the crashing of the waves against the shore, creating a wild, chaotic blend.

We all turned our backs away from the sea as we tried to shield ourselves from the whipping of the water.

"She said she was going to the Welcome Center and hide in the bushes to see the Merry Maker put the sign there," he said.

"Why would she think that?" I wondered.

"Traditionally, that was where the Merry Maker always put it. And over the last few months, the Merry Maker has really shaken things up, straying from the usual places he puts them. That was why she continued to say the Merry Maker wasn't from here. Traditions are being broken."

"And Hillary doesn't like to stray from tradition," I whispered. "Maybe the Merry Maker is trying to throw everyone off. But I can say that I was online with the Merry Maker going back and forth about the placement of the New Year's holiday sign."

"Which means the probability of the Merry Maker killing Hillary is low." Darren finally spoke up. I thought he'd never defend the position we had to keep quiet about.

"Which makes me want to ask you about the fight you and Hillary had the other day at the shop." I watched as his face paled. "Are you okay? You look a little pasty."

"I'm fine. I just remembered the fight and now I regret it. That was the last time I'd spoken to her that morning. Customers were coming in so they could get their last-minute miniatures, and it was busy. Hillary was begging me to go with her and leave the shop." His nostrils flared. He flipped the hoodie back over his head. I wasn't sure if he was trying to shield himself from the blustery weather or trying not to show how upset he was getting. "I told her I had to grow up. She had to grow up and from now on stop including me in any of her little schemes."

He pretty much told us what Mama had observed.

"We are about to turn thirty years old." He flung a hand at Darren. "I have to take my life seriously and do the thing for living. I chose to stay here for Hillary because I honestly thought she'd grow out of wanting to keep everything the same. After years and years of her not accepting that was the way life was going to be, I started to distance myself from her."

Troy curled in his lip and gnawed on it, looking at Darren from under his brows.

"I couldn't be like you. I couldn't just dump the friendship. I continued to hang out with her a few times a month just to make sure she was okay. I'd hoped for one little change, but the older she got, the more radical she became, and I love the growth here in Holiday Junction. She didn't." He took his finger and swiped it underneath his nose before he put his hands back into his pockets.

"I know she said she was going to destroy the shop so you could be free. Didn't that make you want to do something to stop her?" I asked.

"I told you I didn't kill her. Of course I wasn't going to let her do anything, and my mom said she would have to take matters into her own hands if I didn't stop Hillary from coming into the shop." His eyes grew wide. "But that doesn't mean my mom killed her. She was at home getting ready for the ribbon-cutting ceremony."

He looked beyond us into the woods.

"I don't know what I'm doing. I guess I was on a mission to feel better about her being murdered. I really want to get my hands on who stabbed her." He teared up. "I think if she had changed a few years ago, I might've married her."

"I'm sorry, man. I feel horrible about skipping out on our group, but like you said, I knew I'd have to grow up, and when the jiggle joint came up for sale, I jumped at it." Darren, in his own way, apologized.

"Jiggle joint?" That put a smile on Troy's face.

"That's what I call it." I shimmied my shoulders like one of the dancers on the bar's stage.

"Why don't you come by one night and have a round on the house?" Darren and Troy shook hands before Troy took off toward the boat slips near the pier.

After Troy was far enough away, I told Darren, "I'm so glad he gave up on going into the woods."

"Me too."

"Where's he going now?" I asked.

"His boat. He lives out there," Darren told me. As we walked back up to the street, he recalled Troy's past. "He and his mom really didn't get along all that well. He had this boat he'd restored, and when they fought, he'd leave the house to go fix it up. From what I've heard, he lives between his boat and his mom's house."

"Mama can be hard to live with sometimes, but I love her." I couldn't help but think of Mama and me when I was growing up. "Millie Kay took mothering very seriously."

I liked it when I made Darren laugh.

"It was like a job to her. And well, I do love her for it." I twirled around with my head up to the sky and my mouth open to try to catch the snowflakes. "I turned out perfect."

"Perfect, huh?" Darren winked. "I think we need to go see Denise. She would greatly benefit with Hillary out of her hair."

Darren became all business again. I wondered if he saw this as a way to win his dad over or at least have something in common with the man, but I kept my mouth closed. He would open up when he wanted to. He'd proven to do that more and more as we'd spent time together.

"The reason is obvious, but it sounds like you have a deeper motive than just destroying the shop." I coaxed him to elaborate. "I still have coffee." I held the box of coffee up in the air.

We turned around and headed back toward the seaside.

"Troy is the Kenners' only son." Darren and I both continued to walk up the street, constantly moving our bodies in the opposite direction of the bitter cold wind.

Larger flakes of snow were starting to fall and resting on top of the layers of snow that had accumulated over the past few days.

"Standing there talking to him, my childhood memories of being at his house flooded back to me. Denise always said that Troy had to marry someone who was going to enjoy the shop and be more than happy to care of her when she was older. Hillary was not that." We took a sharp right onto the sidewalk, making our way toward Ceramic Celebration. "I remembered something we needed to check on—she told me privately once that she wanted me to stop being friends with Hillary because it would make Troy want to do what I did."

"You mean she was telling you back then to dump the friendship?" I asked. He nodded. "You didn't, did you?"

"No. I just played off her comment, and she never mentioned it again. I didn't say a word to Troy, but it wasn't too long after her saying that to me that I did break away from the friendships. I'd gotten more and more into the fiddle instead of guitars. I had to do some odd jobs around town to pay for it. Not Rhett. He had already decided he was going to be a contractor and buy up all the run-down buildings, houses, whatever structures and bring them back to life. My dad didn't like me taking up the fiddle." More emotions hid behind the words, but I wasn't going to press him on them. "A person can only take so much from someone until they explode."

Darren reached out and held the handle of Ceramic Celebration's door.

My face immediately felt the heat from the inside, but my mind was chilled at the thought that Darren's statement might hold more meaning than just his history with Denise Kenner.

CHAPTER SIXTEEN

Ceramic Celebration's front area had a counter where customers could purchase items or ask questions. The area also included display cases with finished pottery pieces for sale.

The workshop area was in the far back with pottery wheels, kilns, and other equipment used for creating and firing pottery. Some customers were sitting at tables, working on projects. Not too far from them lay a storage area for clay, glazes, and other supplies.

A gallery of sorts, displaying finished pottery pieces, was along the right wall. With my hands clasped so I didn't accidentally knock anything off, I walked along the wall, admiring the work.

I noticed a slightly open door with a sign marked Employees Only. I glanced inside and saw paperwork and files piled up on a desk.

Darren had gone off to find Denise while I continued to glance around the shop.

There were plenty of sinks that could possibly be where Denise—um, the killer—washed their hands. When I peeked over the sink tubs, all I saw were pieces of clay and different stains of paint.

Next to the cleanup station were two doors marked Bathroom.

"Darren!" I heard someone call his name.

I whipped around to see a woman with shoulder-length gray hair and an apron scurrying across the floor with her arms wide open. "I'm so happy to see you."

As I made my way over to them, I watched Darren's expression to gauge his reaction to her. By the way his smile didn't reach his eyes, I could see he truly thought she could be Hillary's killer.

"Let me do the talking," he said in a sort of warning tone as she gained speed.

"Look at you." Denise bounced up on the toes of her shoes and wrapped her arms around his neck.

"Happy New Year," Darren greeted her, bending down to her level with a slightly loose hug back.

I'd come to learn that Darren never said words just to make someone feel good, and he didn't tell Denise that it was good to see her too.

"This is the new editor at *Junction Journal*." He pointed at me. "Violet Rhinehammer. Of course Mom wants to give you some spotlight for the mini-village, and I told her I'd bring Violet down here to get an interview since I wanted to stop in and wish you a happy New Year."

"You're the sweetest." She pinched his cheek and turned to me. "I wish my boy turned out like this one."

"He's a real nice guy." I grinned back at her, trying not to judge her about her son. Troy seemed perfectly fine to me. After all, he'd done exactly what she'd expected him to do.

Give up his life for her.

"Your mother is always thinking of all of our shops in town." She curled her hand around Darren's bicep and guided him past me, across the floor of the shop, and back to the counter, where there was a single stool.

She literally pushed him down to make him sit on it, leaving me to stand.

"Violet even stopped by Brewing Beans to get your favorite brew." Darren took the cups and the box of coffee from me. He poured a cup for Denise and one for himself.

I declined when he offered me one.

"What's your questions?" She ran her hand down her dirty apron, clicking off dried pieces of clay. "Are we taking a photo? Because I'll need to comb my hair." She put her hands around the cardboard cup.

"Sure. But it can wait. We will get the questions out of the way," I told her and took out my phone. Darren got up and offered the stool to me, and I took it.

"He's such a gentleman." Denise smirked and winked at him.

I sucked in a deep breath to gain my composure, thinking of how she might react after I start peppering her with questions. A mix of earthy and claylike scents curled up in my nose.

The warmth of the kilns radiated through the shop, making a faint smell of sawdust fill the air from the wooden-handled tools and various equipment the customers were using.

Overall, the smell of Ceramic Celebration was unique and inviting. No wonder Mama felt encouraged to explore the creative process of making pottery and contributing to the mini-village.

"Do you mind if I use the voice recorder? I like to take the interviews back to the office and type them up. Make sure I don't misquote you or anything." I had no intentions of putting an article in the paper about Ceramic Celebration, but if that was the angle Darren thought we should take, then I was going with it.

We'd have to decide later what we did with whatever information she gave us.

"Can you tell me about the mini-village and how Ceramic Celebration has played a part in that over the years?" I gave her softball questions to start off with.

As she told the story, I wasn't invested in the answer because more and more real questions about how she could've played a role in Hillary's murder grew louder in my mind.

I let her ramble for at least three minutes. It was when my face started to hurt from my fake smile that I decided to throw the first real question out there.

"Also in the history of the mini-village is the change in Holiday Junction. The added tourism," I continued, watching as she shifted uncomfortably, busying her hands with an order pad that sat on the small counter. "One citizen in particular hasn't been able to deal with much change and really focused on ruining the mini-village. All the pieces that come from here."

My shoulders twisted as I gestured around the shop.

"Hillary Stevens. I believe you know her." I gave Denise a hard stare.

"I do. Did." Her few words held a bitterness. "She was a nuisance that apparently wronged someone too many times."

Interesting choice of words.

"Can you tell me the last time you'd seen Hillary?" I asked.

"I thought this was an article about the shop." Denise didn't shoot her question at me. She asked Darren.

"It is. But it's also about what's going on currently," Darren whispered. "Between us, my dad is looking into your shop, and if we can get a positive article out there before he gets here, then…" Darren let the incomplete sentence linger and toggled his hand back and forth.

"You were always looking out for me." She giggled and dragged her hand down his arm.

"How does your husband feel about this shop?" I asked, hoping to remind her to get her paws off Darren.

"There's no husband." She offered me a curt smile. "But if you want to know about Hillary, there's not much to say. The girl was always a pain. I'd never want anything to happen to her, but we all knew she was going to get into some sort of trouble that would lead to something like this."

"According to the initial autopsy, Hillary was stabbed somewhere, and then her body was placed at the scene," I said. Denise's face stilled. I continued, "She was murdered early in the morning, and I know Troy was here that morning and confronted her here."

"How do you know that?" She looked me over with a critical eye.

"My mama is Millie Kay, and she was a witness." I continued to watch her body language as her shoulders fell a little, softening her stance.

"You're Millie Kay's daughter," she said with a snort. "I do think she mentioned that she was working at the paper for her daughter, but it didn't mean anything at the time."

"Where were you the early morning of the murder?" I asked.

"I was at home getting ready for the ribbon-cutting ceremony." She spat out the same thing Troy told us verbatim.

"That was what Troy said, word for word." It made me quickly ask, "Would he do anything to protect you?"

"I don't think I like what you're trying to say." She pulled back her shoulders and stood up straight. "This interview is over." She used air quotes around "interview."

"I'm sorry, but really we need to know the details so we can get to Dad before he comes in here. Creating a scene isn't good for business." Darren patted his chest. "I should know. Dad tried to take the jiggle joint away from me that time, and I wasn't well prepared. I want you to be ready."

"See." She laid a hand on his chest. "This is why I say you're one of a kind. That heart of yours." She looked at Darren with obvious admiration. Her jaw clenched when she turned back to me. "Like I said, I was at home getting ready for the ribbon-cutting ceremony. Before the ceremony, I went to Brewing Beans to get a cup of my favorite seasonal blend from Hazelynn."

"The crème brûlée." I lifted the cup and took a drink.

My mind turned to the hot liquid going down her throat like poison for the lie she just told me. Hazelynn told me Denise had yet to come in, so why was she lying?

I kept it to myself. There was no way I wanted to upset the apple cart again if Darren was unable to smooth it over.

"Anyone else able to confirm you were home and you went to Brewing Beans?" I asked.

"I live alone." Her tone indicated she didn't like the question.

"I need some real answers if I'm going to be able to make sure your name is clear. It's a known fact you wanted Hillary out of your business and your life. Darren has told me all about his friend history with Troy and Hillary." I looked down at the phone to make sure it was still recording. "I mean if she continued to come in here and cause problems, it would run off customers, particularly if she kept breaking customers' mini-village pieces.

"Have you ever heard the term 'the juice ain't worth the squeeze'?" I questioned. "I think customers wouldn't want to come back in, which would make you lose business, especially if word got around about the little problem. Hillary." I snorted. "How else would you pay your bills?"

The bell over the door dinged.

We all looked to see who was coming into the shop.

Troy's eyes locked with mine.

"I told you what we knew. Now get out." He rushed across the shop, flinging the hood off his head. "We didn't kill her."

"I felt sorry for the poor girl and even offered her a job. She took it." Denise really got my attention.

"She worked here?" I twisted around to look at Troy.

"Up until a few days ago. We had to let her go because she was harassing customers about the mini-village. She swore when we offered her the job she wouldn't make trouble." Troy started to tell the truth behind the argument they'd had, the one Mama had witnessed. "The other day, she went crazy after Gail Steinner had completed her project, and I had to kick her out."

"Gail Steinner. The teacher?" I asked. Quickly, I said, "The one who made the huge Rapunzel castle?"

"That's right." Denise nodded. "She sat right over there."

My eyes followed her finger and landed square on the wall behind a table. If you didn't look closely enough, you'd think the shelving was filled with painted pottery ready for the kiln. But a small part of one shelf had pottery tools on it.

One stood out.

"What is that tool?" I asked and walked across the room to pick it up.

The wood handle was attached to a long steel rod with a pointy end.

"It's a pottery tool called an awl." Troy's words pierced my ears as the images of the wound in Hillary's autopsy report pretty much told me this was the type of weapon Chief Strickland and Curtis were looking for. "What?" he asked, picking up one of the tools. "They are used for various types of things, like carving designs into clay, like this piece."

He reached on the shelf and picked up a clay castle.

"One of our regulars, the art teacher at school, has been working on a castle for months. She's used the smaller pointed awl to create all the bricks so they can be carved out to look as real as possible." He pointed at what he was talking about, but my insides swirled around like the second hand on the clock on the wall above his head.

"Did she make the Rapunzel piece displayed in the mini-village?" I asked.

"She did." Troy nodded. "Why?"

Denise grabbed her heart and gasped. "It was Gail's piece Hillary was tied to."

The color fell from her face, making her look more like a ghost from this past Halloween than someone who was ready to ring in the new year.

"If you know something about Gail that could possibly pertain to Hillary's murder, I'm asking you to please tell me," Darren said to Denise.

"Mom, you always say to keep our noses out of it. I think it best we do that—tell them what we know." Troy set the mini-castle and the awl back on the shelf. "They are working with Darren's dad."

"I need to come clean." I offered a smile, hoping she'd find some sort of connection that made her feel like she could tell me the information bubbling up in her like a shaken bottle of champagne about to pop its cork. "We are looking into things for the police department but using the angle of the newspaper to get people to talk to us."

"I know this seems devious. But we thought with your history of how you felt about Hillary, you wouldn't tell us the truth. I'm sorry for that." Darren's sincere apology must've fallen upon her heart.

"Hillary and I were here one night a few months ago." Troy looked at his mom and then back at us. "Gail would come in each afternoon after school, which was when she'd work on the project. She continued to make her addition to the mini-village better and better. Most people who enter the contest just come in a couple of times and they are done. Not Gail."

"No. She wanted to win so bad because the prize is a full year of free groceries. Gail has a lot of children she sees in her class that come in hungry. Their families barely have enough money to put a little food on the table, much less nutritious food." Denise's voice broke.

"Go on, Mom," Troy encouraged her.

"Her story was so touching, I decided to help her with her Rapunzel mini-castle. I wondered why she'd want to add such a thing to the mini-village, and she said it was because the children in her class loved the fairy tale so much. The idea of escaping the poverty level they had like Rapunzel escaped the evil witch who took her."

Though it wasn't quite the same, I could see how children could hear the story and want a better life for themselves.

"Like Troy mentioned, he and Hillary were in here, and so was Gail. The more she told the story about why she wanted to win, the angrier Hillary got about the whole idea of putting a Rapunzel castle in the mini-village because it wasn't like Holliday Junction was some fairy tale." Her disapproving expression told me exactly how she'd felt about Hillary.

"Are you saying Gail killed Hillary?" I would not have been shocked if they did think this because I'd already concluded she could be a suspect, since Hillary's hair was tied to Gail's piece.

"I'm saying Hillary broke in here that night and destroyed every single piece Gail had made." Denise just gave me a perfect motive for killing Hillary. "She also had the tools to do it with since we placed an order for her so she could take some of the clay pieces and work on them at school during her lunch break or the children's recess."

Darren and I looked at each other.

"We called your father, and they sent someone to take a report," Denise said.

My brows winged up.

Not only did we have a good motive, but we also had a weapon.

CHAPTER SEVENTEEN

"**D**ad." Denise let Darren take an awl from the shop so we could take an example to the police station. "This has to be the murder weapon." Darren put it on the chief's desk. "Gail Steinner is the killer. I'm sure if you go to the shop and take all the awls or even go to Gail's and see if she's got an awl, you'll have to find some sort of trace of blood that's seeped into the wood or something."

Chief Strickland picked it up and looked at it from all angles.

"Yes, sir," I said. "Initially, we thought Troy might've killed Hillary because their friendship had soured, but when we confronted him, he had an alibi, so we naturally went to look into his mom."

"Denise Kenner?" Matthew looked at me with the tired eyes of a middle-aged man who'd not gotten any sleep over the past few nights. He snorted. "I've known Denise all my life. That woman doesn't have a mean bone in her body. Just because she owns Ceramic Celebration, where all the people who entered the mini-village contest did all their work, doesn't mean she killed the girl."

"She did have or does have motive. Hillary was breaking and entering the shop, destroying everyone's pieces. Denise said she'd called you and that a report was made." I continued to talk while Matthew pulled files out of a drawer and started to thumb through them. "Denise most certainly had motive if everything in her shop was getting destroyed and people had to come back in to remake their things or even decided not to remake them or ever come back to the shop. That would stop all income, which would affect everyone's bottom line and cost of living."

I glared at the man, who seemed to ignore me. He pulled out one file after another, opened it, and put it back, never once glancing up at me.

"I'd say if someone was messing with my livelihood, then I'd want to get rid of them too." I decided to try a different approach since he seemed to refuse to listen to why the friend he'd known all his life could possibly do something like this. "Maybe it was an accident. Maybe Denise did catch Hillary in the act of breaking in and stabbed her out of sheer madness. Once she realized what she'd done, she moved her to the mini-village and made it look as though Gail Steinner had done it because of their history."

"Wait." That got Matthew's attention. "I thought you said this was the murder weapon and Gail Steinner did it. But now you're telling me Denise Kenner filed a report a few months ago about Hillary breaking in and giving me motive for her to have killed Hillary."

"Oh." I suddenly realized I'd not given a reason for Gail to have killed Hillary, which was where Darren and I had thought this was going.

Matthew grunted like he was going to say something, but he didn't. He pushed the filing drawer shut and clasped his hands together before laying them on his desk.

"Why do you think Gail Steinner did it?" Matthew seemed genuinely interested in what Darren and I had discovered.

After we told him what Denise had told us about Gail and her reason for wanting to win, he sat back in his chair and gnawed on his cheek as he thought about our theory.

"And Denise told you she made a police report about Hillary Stevens breaking into her store?" he asked.

Darren and I nodded. I patted around for my phone so I could play the recording, and then I realized Darren and I had rushed out of the shop so fast, I'd left my phone there.

"Thank you for the information." Matthew sat up and scooted to the edge of the desk chair. With his palms flat on the desk, he pushed himself up to stand. "I'm going to check into Gail's alibi, but first I'm going to get with Curtis to see if this could be a possible murder weapon."

He shuffled Darren and me out quickly. It felt very strange, and I'd kept my mouth shut until we made it back outside, where the snow had started to come down even more.

It was nice to have snow on Christmas, but New Year's was a time I felt was renewal. Holiday Junction needed that renewal, which meant I had only a couple of days as the time ticked off the current year to bring the killer to justice. And the snow.

It, too, needed to go away.

"Did you think my dad was acting odd?" Darren brought it up before I could.

"Yes. He was occupied with the files." I tugged the edges of my coat up around my neck, grateful I'd worn my hair down because it covered my ears and neck, making the cold somewhat bearable while we walked along the sidewalk toward the main part of town.

"Those files are printed copies of the dispatch calls they get in, and I'm worried he's forgetting what calls he goes on." Darren led the way as we walked and talked.

"You think he's getting too old?" I didn't think Matthew was old, but I also didn't know him very well.

"I think he's got a full plate, and he just does. Once he's done with one task, he puts it out of his head and moves on to the next." I listened to him talk.

"Maybe he wanted to remember the full dispatch and add that to the case." I shrugged. "I've got to get back to the office. Mae is there, and I've got a newspaper to get out."

I pointed ahead at the trolley stop, where a few people had already gathered around the propane heating lamps the Village Council had put out around town. It was nice to be able to walk around and take in the glitter and glitz they'd spat out all over Holiday Junction in anticipation of the Sparkle Ball.

"I'll be in touch." Darren had other things on his mind he'd not disclosed. "I've got band practice tonight, so I might not see you until tomorrow."

"Oh." I found it cute that he was giving me his schedule as if he knew that I'd question his silence if I didn't hear from him in a certain time, which was true. "That's going to be exciting. Me at the Sparkle Ball watching you on stage ring in the new year."

"It's a good time." The words trailed behind him as he continued to walk, leaving me at the trolley stop.

He didn't act as though he was going to ring in the new year with the traditional kiss at midnight.

Not that we would, but a girl could wish.

As I got on the trolley, I reminded myself it was going to be a New Year, and I wondered what it would look like for me not only living here in Holiday Junction but with Darren.

"What's got you all lit up?" Goldie Bennett's head tilted, making her glitter-ball earrings shine in my eyes.

"Just the prospect of a new year." I eased into the seat behind hers. "Don't you love the feeling this time every year at the idea of new, fresh starts?"

"Not when there's a killer on the loose." She slammed the lever, closing the trolley door. She glanced back in her big rearview mirror to make sure everyone was holding on before she sped away from the town's business district. "Where are you headed?"

"The office." I sat back and watched the town drift by as we passed the shops and headed back out of town, where I got lost in my thoughts of what it would be like if Darren jumped offstage and swept me up into his arms at the stroke of midnight, his fiddle down at his side.

My heart tickled, and I coughed a little.

"You aren't getting sick, are you?" Goldie asked.

"No. Just clearing my throat." The dream faded away the closer we got to the office. My thoughts went back to the real-life issue. Hillary Stevens.

"I saw your friend today. She hitched a ride to the Welcome Center and then back to your office." Goldie knew all the town gossip. "I couldn't help but overhear her talking to someone on the phone, telling them all about Hillary Stevens."

"I bet she was talking to Hank, her boyfriend." I pulled my bag closer to my body and wondered what he'd suggested we do about Hillary's murder. "He's a private investigator back home."

"Huh. We could use one of them here." Goldie was right about that.

"Excuse me." Another passenger sitting across from me had gotten Goldie's attention. They'd asked her about some sightseeing things, and while she told them all about Holiday Junction, I sat back and waited for my stop.

"I'll see you later," I called when I stepped off the trolley to the unofficial stop along her route. She dumped me off there at the small walk-up to the cottage.

I thought about Rhett's mention that Hillary didn't like me making changes to the cottage. Motives to kill her were all over the place, ranging from the historic district to the founding fathers. So many people with motive.

"Honey, I'm home," I trilled when I stepped into the office and took off my coat, which I hung on the coatrack next to the door.

"Get in here!" Mama called from her office. "Doesn't Mae look as pretty as a speckled pup?"

I walked into Mama's office, where she and Mae were posing in their matching gold lamé jumpsuits.

"Oh my." My eyes grew, as did my smile. "You two look like you're ready for the Sparkle Ball."

"Your mama was so kind to get me and you an outfit to match hers," Mae said through her gritted teeth just beyond her fake grin.

"I saw you eyeballing it." Mama had probably misread the horror on Mae's face when Mae was looking at it.

"Here." Mama held out a bag with the Bubbly Boutique's logo on the front. "I paid a little extra so you and Mae can go in there today while I'm at the Leading Ladies practice and add some dash and dazzle."

Mama dramatically twisted her wrist as she wiggled the bag in in front of her for me to take. The little extras she was talking about were like the bracelets she was nonchalantly trying to show off.

"You're too kind, Mama." I took the bag and peeked inside. "My very own gold lamé jumpsuit. Goody."

"I knew you were going to love it." Mama flickered her fingers at the door. "Now you two go in there and get whatever work you need to do done so we can get on our way. Our credit cards are crying to be raked through the machines."

"I'm kinda liking it." Mae was such a liar. "And I am going to wear it proud because I don't have to live here."

"That's why you don't care." I sucked in a deep breath and sat down at the desk. "I need to run all the clues about Hillary while you sit there and listen."

"Listen?" Mae reached across my desk and grabbed a piece of paper. "Can I use this to write things down on?" She searched around the penholder until she settled on a pencil and sat down. "This is how the Laundry Club Ladies and I do it."

She proceeded to tell me all the secret little details about her and the little group of five she'd formed back home. They worked together as amateur sleuths to solve local crimes. It was a group I'd tried to get in a few times when I lived there, but my tactics held them back from asking me to join.

But that was when I made my own side deal with Mae. The "I'll help you out if you help me out" kind of way. A few times, we put our heads together to get clues. Now that there was distance between us, and I'd called her for advice a few times, we'd become friends to some degree.

"We have Berta." I started to go down the road that Berta had her own motive to have killed Hillary, except Mae stopped me.

"Dead end." She wrote Berta's name on top of the piece of paper and crossed it out. Then she wrote Alibi in all capital letters. "I went there today to check out the crime scene for myself. She was there trying to clean up the mess the police department had made so they could open the mini-village tomorrow after they announced the winner. She was eating at the Freedom Diner that morning with a group of Village Council members."

"Okay. What about the founding father families who are on the council?" I knew we'd talked about them. "The Bristols and the Kenners we can mark off because they were all there."

"Denise Kenner told me she was at home." I narrowed my eyes.

"Troy was there. Not Denise." Mae's curly honey-blond hair bounced as her voice picked up. "Definitely look into Denise still."

"Right. She has the motive of her dream of her son going to college, which he didn't because he and Hillary were an undisclosed item. Also, Hillary continually broke into Ceramic Celebration and broke all the crafts and minis anyone made. If that wasn't enough motive, the financial stress that put on the shop was." I rattled off what I'd learned over the course of the last twenty-four hours. Mae tried to keep up and write it all down.

"And I found the murder weapon," I stated with confidence, though I'd not gotten confirmation of it from Matthew.

Mae's eyes widened. She opened her mouth then snapped it shut.

"Right?" I nodded, agreeing with her facial expression. "It's an awl. A tool they use in Ceramic Celebration."

"That would explain the length." Mae opened the file sitting on my desk. We'd been placing little bits and pieces of information in there. She pointed at the photo Matthew had given us, which had been taken at Hillary's autopsy. "It was just long enough to penetrate the liver and bladder. Killing her. Plus the hole where the stab wound was would match that of the tip of an awl."

"Exactly."

"What about fingerprints?" Mae asked. I grimaced. "On the weapon."

"I didn't find the actual murder weapon," I clarified, even though Mae's shoulders had already slumped forward. "I was at Ceramic Celebration and saw the tool, immediately recognizing it could be the weapon. Denise has all of them at her disposal. So it has to be in there somewhere."

"In the pottery shop?" Mae asked. "Where Denise wiped it clean?"

"Let's hope it's not all clean," I suggested, knowing good and well Denise cleaned each tool after a crafter used it. "Darren and I stopped in at the police station to tell his dad."

She beamed at the mere mention of Darren's name.

I gave her a sarcastic look. "Now is not the time to even bring that up."

"Okay, so Denise is definitely our main suspect," she said flatly. "Who's next?"

"Gail Steinner." I couldn't forget the teacher and her history with Hillary.

"Did I hear you say Gail Steinner?" The slam of the front door that followed that question was so hard, the windows rattled before the woman who asked it appeared at the door of the office. "I'm Hillary Stevens's mother, and I hear you might be able to help me more than the sloppy police."

"Yes, ma'am, we can." Mae immediately jumped up and greeted Mrs. Stevens. "I'm Mae West, and this is Violet Rhinehammer. We are so sorry for your loss. The community's loss of such a fine woman who loved her village so much."

"She did. That was what got her in trouble." The woman had sleek gray hair with a pair of pressed trousers and a purple coat. "We told her she had to stop being so perfect. Let the town grow and grow with it, but she insisted that the world outside of Holiday Junction was changing too fast."

"Let me get you a water while Violet gets some information from you." Mae excused herself, leaving me alone with Mrs. Stevens.

"Like Mae said, I've been really diving into this case." My heart sank as I took in her up-close features. From a distance, she looked put together, but the closer she got, the deeper the dark circles under her eyes and the lines around her lips were.

A true picture of grief. Loss.

"One of my employees, Prudence, told me you'd come into Cup of Cheer." Mrs. Stevens looked between Mae and me. "I'm here to ask you to pay a visit to Gail Steinner, but if I heard correctly when I walked inside, you already have her on your list."

She eyeballed the notes Mae had been taking.

"I don't believe Denise would kill Hillary. Denise is Hillary's godmother, and anytime Hillary wreaked havoc on the shop and even when Troy decided to stay in town after high school, Denise and I would get together for coffee at Brewing Beans to discuss the situation. Hillary's bark was worse than her bite. She would get mad and then immediately apologize to Denise. I paid for any damages," she said.

"You don't think Hillary's activities had reached Denise's boiling point?" I had to be frank with Mrs. Stevens. "Everyone has a boiling point. Even my preacher back home where I grew up ended up killing someone and going to prison." I shook my head. "Not even his direct line to Jesus stopped him."

"Heavens no." Mrs. Stevens's eyes filled with water. She looked off into the distance and blinked back a memory. Her grief had found an escape through the tears that fell gently down her face and grew larger and larger. "Like I said, Denise and I have been friends for a long time. If anyone had motive, it was Gail."

I reached to the other side of my desk, plucked a couple of tissues out of the box, then walked them and the box over to her.

"Thank you," she whispered and used them to dry her face. She glanced up at Mae with a smile of gratitude and took the glass of water. "Gail and Hillary got into a fight a few days ago. Hillary didn't like the portrayal of Rapunzel Gail was making. I know it seems silly for Hillary to even care what others did, but she was just so upset when she felt like Gail was making it seem that Holiday Junction needed to be saved like Rapunzel."

"You mentioned Prudence told you about us coming into Cup of Cheer." I waited for her to nod and confirm I'd heard her correctly when she first came into the cottage. "Did she mention to you that she told me she suspected Berta?"

"She didn't, but I could see why she'd think that." Mrs. Stevens took a sip of the water. "Berta is a sheep in wolf's clothing. She has come in several times threatening to do something about Hillary on her own, but she doesn't."

She took one last drink before she got to her feet.

"Speaking of Cup of Cheer, I saw that the Merry Maker picked your shop to host the end of the last party of the year." I watched her closely to see what her body language told me about her real reaction to the placement, since it was Darren's idea.

It almost warmed my heart to see my question had brought a faint smile to her face.

"Hillary would've loved that." Her voice faded to a hushed stillness as though she were picturing how her daughter would've reacted. "It would've restored her belief the Merry Maker was in fact a person who lived in Holiday Junction instead of this crazy notion she'd gotten a few months ago that it was an outsider."

"Hillary really loved Holiday Junction." I couldn't believe it was Darren Strickland's idea that would've changed Hillary's mind. He was going to love this.

"She did. Unfortunately, I do believe it was her downfall. Don't think I didn't hear our neighbors talk about Hillary as a nuisance, but if it weren't for her, the mini-village would've never been dusted off after she found it in the storage area of the library." Despite the sadness of the conversation, she chuckled.

"I'm sorry. What?" I asked then quickly clarified what I meant. "It's my understanding the mini-village has always been around and added to each year."

"Yes, but years ago, when Hillary was a baby, the Village Council had decided there really wasn't a place to display it and packaged up the village." What she was saying about storage at the library was true. I'd been in there several times to research articles and various facts I needed for the *Junction Journal*. "I'd had many pieces I was working on, since any free time Denise and I spent playing with the kids, we made pottery. It was just another happy memory Hillary had of her life."

"How did Hillary help out?" Mae asked. She'd gotten the piece of paper a few minutes ago and had been writing away as Mrs. Stevens continued to talk.

"This was around the time the town had decided to really do up the holidays, bring the shops back to life, and bring in tourists. Hillary was in middle school and worked at the library. She shelved books and sometimes read to the children. One day she happened upon the storage area where the mini-village was kept safe." Mrs. Stevens's face lit up.

I could imagine what a little girl would think of a small dollhouse-like find. I loved my dollhouse when I was a little girl.

"She found the replica of our house, which I'd made before she was born, and brought it home with the idea the mini-village could be a wonderful way for Holiday Junction to show the new tourists just how special our town had always been." The way Mrs. Stevens was telling the story made me appreciate the mini-village so much more.

"Obviously, the Village Council loved the idea," I said.

"Oh, they did." Her eyes shot open. "It was a great success, and they praised Hillary for it. There was even a write-up in the *Junction Journal* with a photo of her standing next to it that year."

Mrs. Stevens's face paled as she recalled the next memory.

"It was after that the Village Council came up with the idea to start a contest to add to the village. Hillary couldn't understand why on earth they'd want to add to something that was already so perfect." She sighed and looked down. "That was when Hillary's personality changed to what it became. She took on this role of believing that she had to save the history of the town. No matter what we did—counseling, begging, bribing—she didn't ever change her mind."

Her phone rang from her purse. She dug down in it and pulled the phone out to see who was calling.

"It's my husband. I have to go." She put the glass of water on the desk. "Curtis Robinson is releasing Hillary's body, and we have to make funeral arrangements."

She closed her eyes and shook her head.

"I never thought those words would ever come out of my mouth." Her lips tugged together in a flat line.

"I'm so sorry. It's not natural." Mae patted Mrs. Stevens's back. "We are so very sorry for your loss."

"If that's true…" Mrs. Stevens's voice took on a stern tone. Not a quiver at all. "Then you will find the person who did this to my baby."

Mrs. Stevens walked out, leaving me with an unsettling sensation, an unease as if something was about to happen. I wasn't so sure Denise Kenner was as innocent as Mrs. Stevens thought.

CHAPTER EIGHTEEN

U nfortunately, calls to Holiday Junction School Board had not been answered after many failed attempts to get in touch with someone at the elementary school to see if Gail was there.

The school system was still on winter break, which meant the teachers were probably enjoying their time off.

There were still so many things to do for the paper that I had little time to continue looking into Mrs. Stevens's claims. And New Year's Eve was tomorrow, so it looked like the ending to the year wouldn't be what we'd hoped it was going to be.

A killer behind bars.

"What do you think we should do?" Mae asked as she continued to press the green call button on her phone. She had some crazy idea someone was at the school and eventually would pick up if she kept calling. "Someone has to be there—a janitor, anyone."

"We aren't looking for just anyone." I reminded her. "We are looking for this woman."

I turned my computer monitor around to show her the online yearbook photo I'd found of Gail Stevens after an online search proved to be fruitless.

"The woman is not on any sort of social media, and though she and

Hillary had words, it doesn't appear that she's done anything but be accused of being someone who cares for her students." I did find an article in the *Junction Journal* archives about her winning the Teacher of the Year award years ago.

"I think we need to find out where she lives and just show up." I had an idea. "I do believe I can look at the database to see who has an online account with the *Junction Journal*." I typed away.

"I do love how you think, Violet Rhinehammer." This wasn't the first time I'd heard Mae say that to me. Only the first time since she'd been here.

"Steinner," I said slowly as I typed it into the subscription page to bring up her account. "Voilà."

Mae leaned in and squinted as she went back and forth between looking at the address and writing it down on her piece of paper.

"Got it!" Her voice rose with excitement. "Let's go."

I started laughing so hard I doubled over.

"What?" Mae asked. "What's wrong with you?"

"Me," I snorted through tears. "Me and…" I choked through the ugly laughter and pointed between us.

I swung myself up to stand and lifted my eyes to the ceiling as I took in a deep breath.

"Only me and you would be excited to find the address of a potential killer. That tickled my funny bone." I powered down my computer and followed Mae to the door, where we both grabbed our coats before we headed out.

"I think Dottie is right." Mae curled her arm in my elbow. "Violet Rhinehammer must've lost her mind to leave Normal."

"Honey, I'm the sanest one." I smiled and shifted my focus. "We've got to get to Gail Steinner's, and I don't have a car."

"You know…" Mae stopped. "I didn't even realize you didn't have a car. I hadn't thought about it because the town was so compact."

"The trolley also makes it easy to get around as well." I knew we were getting close to the end of the day, and the trolley would stop running for the night. "I know we could get Goldie to take us, but I'm not sure we'd get a ride back."

Both of us looked back at the golf cart tucked up to the side of the cottage.

"Millie Kay?" Mae asked at the same time as I said "Mama."

Both of us laughed and turned back to go in and see if Mama would either let us drive her golf cart or drive us herself.

"You know I'm in!" Mama didn't skip a beat when we asked her to be our wingman for a ride to Gail's house. "We might'swell lock up for the rest of the day and start our holiday time off a little early."

Mama shut down her computer, grabbed her purse, and switched off the lights in her office. Mae waited out in the hall while I closed everything down. Tomorrow was New Year's Eve, and the office was technically closed, but I had my laptop if I needed to add more items to the online paper. The weekly print version of the paper was long sent off to the local printing shop.

Mama continued to make sure all the other lights in the cottage were turned off and the heat was turned down so it wasn't running while we were gone the next few days.

"I really am having fun," I overheard Mae telling Mama on their way to the golf cart while I locked up the front door of the cottage.

"I'm so glad. You know Violet just works all the time, and not that trying to find out who killed Hillary isn't work, but it's kinda fun, and that's what you two do best," Mama said. She waited for me to unzip the plastic enclosure around the golf cart so we could get in.

"This is awfully fancy, Millie Kay." Mae got in the front seat of the two-bench-seated vehicle. She clipped the lap seat belt around her.

"And we have heat." Mama spared no expense when she bought the golf cart. "Eventually, Violet is going to have to realize she needs one. It's the only way people get around town. And there are even golf cart lots."

"The neighborhoods are so tight that most of them don't have their own driveways," I called from the back bench seat above the whiz of the golf cart's motor and the hum of the heater. "In the subdivisions, every so often there's a small parking lot for golf cart parking for visitors."

"But the owners have a small garage to keep the golf carts in." Mama knew the general area where Denise lived but not the exact house. She'd been all over Holiday Junction and knew it better than I did. "Luckily for me, I bought a house on one of the original streets, which gave me a little land. I have the garage that Violet turned into her home and a garage attached to the house, where I keep my golf cart and Violet's daddy's."

"I'm looking forward to seeing him tonight," Mae said.

Tonight was the night Mama had insisted on cooking for us.

Mama eased past the houses and brought the golf cart to a slow crawl, passing the mailboxes with the house numbers, inching closer and closer to Gail's.

"That's it." I pointed at the house and made a mental note of how far it was from the golf cart parking lot. Mama took the first space there, giving her a clear view of Gail's house, since it was on the opposite side of the street.

"Are you ready?" Mae turned around and held her belly. "I'm a little nervous."

"Not me." I grabbed a couple of business cards from my bag and put them in my coat pocket.

The noise of the zipper teeth as the golf cart cover separated was drowned out by the sound of the snowflakes rustling and crunching under the tires of other vehicles passing. The cover itself made a soft *swoosh* inside as it unzipped. The fabric was slightly wet from the snow.

The snowflakes became more visible as I stepped outside the golf cart. The sound of the snowfall intensified, as did my beating heart.

The anticipation of what Mae and I were about to uncover began to settle into my gut as the nervous tickle surged through my veins.

"Let's go." My words were soft as if I was disturbing the peaceful atmosphere of the cold winter day.

"I'm ready." Mae and I forged across the street. Without hesitation, we walked straight up to Gail's front door and gave it a few hard knocks.

A woman in her late forties to early fifties with graying hair styled in a bob opened the door. She pushed her glasses up on her nose as the wrinkles around her eyes deepened along with her smile. She wore a sweatshirt with some clumps of clay dried on it.

"Can I help you?" she asked.

"Gail Steinner?" I asked to make sure.

She nodded and smiled. There was a bit of confusion on her end as her eyes shifted between Mae and me.

"I'm Violet Rhinehammer, and this is my friend Mae West." I gave her one of my business cards. She took it, and when she read it, her brows rose.

"Junction Journal." Her eyes grew big. "Do I have time to fix my hair?" Excitement spewed out of her, and she patted her hands around her hair. "I can't believe this."

She turned and took a couple of steps into her home. The storm door smacked close between us.

She turned back to us and opened the door.

"Oh, dear me, please come in." Her lips twitched over her nervous laughter. "Please don't print that. Forgive my rudeness, but I just can't believe it."

Mae and I followed her through the entryway into the house and down the hall into another room, which had a sectional couch filled with a lot of pillows. A cat was nestled there before it got up and made its way over to the end table, where it stared us down.

"Mr. Frisky, we did it." Gail patted the cat on the head and disappeared into what I barely saw was a bathroom before she closed the door halfway. "I'll be right out."

"Hi, Mr. Frisky." Mae was a sucker for any animal. "Aren't you the cutest?"

"He sure is." I couldn't help but be a smidge nosy and scan along the bookshelves, where there were some awards Gail had received. "Do you think she was acting odd?"

I ran a finger along the brass plate of the Teacher of the Year award.

"I find this entire town weird." Mae had picked up Mr. Frisky and snugged him close.

"I'm ready," Gail announced. I jumped around so she didn't see me snooping, and Mae had put Mr. Frisky on the floor.

"Wow." I blinked a few times. "You've really fixed yourself up."

Her hair had been taken out of the hair clip and styled in loose curls. Her pale lips had bold red lipstick to match her red statement earrings. The sweatshirt she had worn had been changed for a sleek black jumpsuit with a deep V-neckline and wide-leg pants. She'd paired the jumpsuit with silver strappy heels.

"This is going to help so many families," she said with pride. "I think this will be a great outfit for the photo." She sat down on the chaise lounge next to the couch and crossed her legs. "Wait." She jumped back to her feet, wobbling a little on the heels, but regained her composure fast. "Do you think I should get a glass of champagne?"

She started off in a different direction of the house before she twirled around.

"No. It's for the kids, and I'm not going to drink in front of the kids." She came back to the chaise. "I'm ready now." She swung her head back, and it appeared that she was trying to fluff her hair.

"I wouldn't say it was going to help the Stevenses." My forehead wrinkled. I was confused by her odd behavior.

"Stevenses?" she frowned. "There's not a student with the last name Stevens."

"Hillary Stevens," I told her.

"What does she have to do with the prize?" Gail Steinner was either a good actress or really hadn't heard.

"Prize?" Mae asked.

"I'm sorry, Gail, but I think you believe we're here to let you know you won the mini-village prize." It all added up. She'd mentioned the prize would help families, and I'd heard she was using the year's worth of groceries for a needy student. "We are here to ask you about Hillary

Stevens." She stood up with her arms crossed, a frown etched on her face.

Her eyes were downcast, and she seemed to be lost in thought. As she stood there, she let out a sigh, her shoulders slumped in defeat.

All of a sudden, I felt a sense of guilt or responsibility for the suffering Gail seemed to be having and perceived a strong emotional connection to her.

"I guess you could win," I said, hoping to try to alleviate her suffering look of complete disappointment.

"So I didn't win the mini-village addition or the groceries for a year?" she asked with tears in her eyes. "I was going to give every student's family one of the weeks of groceries. There are fifty-two weeks in the year. They could get two weeks of groceries each. Food on the table, food in their bellies."

"You definitely could've won if Hillary wasn't tied to the castle," Mae said flatly.

"Mae," I scoffed and gave her a hard look. Through my gritted teeth, I said, "She's obviously grieving."

"Don't forget why we are here," Mae said, bringing us back to the investigation. "And we are sorry we aren't here to represent the Holiday Committee, even though Violet's mama is a member. We are here on behalf of the Holiday Junction Police Department."

While Mae told Gail the reason for our visit, I closely watched Gail's emotional roller coaster. You could tell a lot about someone just by reading their body language, and Gail was all over the place in a matter of seconds.

Her brows furrowed and eyes squinted as she tried to process and understand what was happening. Her body tensed as if she was at a loss or unsure of what to do next.

"My castle? She destroyed my castle?" she spat. "That little twit."

Her confusion turned into frustration. As she processed what we were explaining, her eyes grew narrower, her fists clenched into balls, and her voice rose in tone.

"I swear, that girl." She stomped. "It's like those protesters who handcuff themselves to something. Trying to prove a ridiculous point."

"I don't think she tied herself to your castle. According to the autopsy report, she was killed before she was tied to your castle." I took one of the photos—not the one with the wound—from the file and showed it to her.

"Did you say autopsy?" She took the photo. The red rouge on her cheek no longer gave a definition to her face as it once again paled. "Someone tied her hair around my castle and knotted it?"

"Your castle. You had a public fight with Hillary, which was brought to our attention." Mae was going to let Gail know why we believed she had motive.

Gail's hands shook.

"I can't believe you're accusing me of such a heinous crime." Gail paced. She had a hard time making eye contact with us, and her anxious and agitated arms flailed around. "I know what I'm going to do."

She hurried back toward the front door, and Mae and I followed her.

I looked back at Mae, and she could only shrug a shoulder like she didn't know what to do.

"Gail, can we just talk?" I asked.

She flung open a coat closet door and ripped a coat off a hanger. The wooden hanger's edges beat against the wall behind the bar it was hung from. She slammed the door with her toe while she jerked the coat on.

"We are only here to ask you where you were when Hillary was murdered." At least I got her attention, and she stopped shy of the door.

"Where are you going?" I took the moment to ask.

"I'm going to see Matthew Strickland." Her eyes assessed me. "I don't trust journalists. I'm smart enough to know you're trying to get a scoop here by your shifty questions and accusations. I'd not even heard Hillary Stevens is dead."

"It's all over the news," Mae told her.

"I don't have a television. Or did your amazing investigation skills not even notice that when you came into my house under"—she tossed her finger in the air—"what I might add was the false pretense that I won the groceries."

The more she talked, the louder she got, and soon she was yelling.

"You two are the frauds!" she yelled with tight lips, bulging eyes, and flared nostrils. Her face flushed red. "Get out of my house!"

She gave a hard point at the door as her entire body clenched and her jaw tightened.

"So you aren't going to tell us where you were the morning of Hillary Steven's murder?" I gave it another shot. "She was killed with an awl, and from what the Kenners told me, you'd been working a lot with that tool lately."

"I said get out of my house!" Under her screams, Mae and I tucked tail and quickly walked past her.

"I'm sure you were mad when you caught Hillary trying to break your Rapunzel-themed castle. And you wanted so bad for your students to have those full bellies, and you snapped." I did a quick jab with my hand. "You only wanted to stop her, and you didn't know you were going to pierce her liver and," I was about to tell her the rest of the autopsy report, but she gave another go at screaming at us.

"I'll have your jobs for this!" was the last thing Gail said before slamming the door behind us.

"That was that." Mae snickered. "She was a bit scary."

"Yeah." I agreed but got lost in my thoughts while Mae continued to describe how Gail looked more suspicious than we'd previously thought.

"Even if she thought you were there to snoop and do a story on her in the paper about her being a suspect, she should've at least cleared her name." Mae was used to how people acted back home.

It was different here. Most of the people here loved their privacy and tried at all costs to keep it.

Mae was still yammering on about motive. Being the hero by giving free groceries to the families would be a notch on Gail's belt, but I did feel like she truly wanted to be able to provide that with no ego attached.

Mama saw us coming and unzipped the cover.

"She is passionate about her students, and if she caught Hillary at the Welcome Center when she was putting on her final touches, she might've snapped." I got in the back of the golf cart and let Mae sit up there with Mama.

I wanted to think about what just transpired with Gail, and if I sat up front, I'd be thinking about my safety.

"What happened?" Mama twisted around the seat to look at me.

"Millie Kay," Mae said, beginning to laugh, "you would've died. Gail thought we were there to tell her she won the mini-village addition prize. She ran into her bathroom and got all dolled up."

"Tell me everything." Mama's Southern tone dripped, just begging to hear all the details.

"I mean she pulled her hair out of that clip and let it flow in curls. She had on this ratty sweatshirt, but when she came back out of the bathroom, she had on this jumpsuit, and I mean it was…" Mae didn't finish her sentence. She used her fingers to make a dramatic V down her chest.

Mama turned around and sat there, and Mae snickered for a second.

"For a teacher who wanted to give her students food, she might've worn something with a little more coverage," Mae said with her back to me and face forward.

"I think it's odd that she didn't want to even give us a reason and kicked us out without hesitation." I gnawed on the thought she was covering something up, but I wasn't sure what it was.

"Maybe she can tell us." Mama put the golf cart in gear and pointed at Gail leaving her driveaway, taking a quick right turn on the side-walk, and coming toward us. She didn't have on the high heels anymore, and from what I could see peeking out from underneath her coat, she'd exchanged her fancy jumpsuit for more weather-appro-priate clothes.

Mama turned off the golf cart, cutting the engine.

"Slump down or something," Mama cried out as Gail got closer.

None of us tried to hide. We all just turned our heads together in the middle, hoping that if she saw us, she'd think we were different people and in there discussing something.

"Shoo." Mama gasped. "I don't think she noticed us."

"Where do you think she's going?" Mae asked.

"The police station. She said she was going to go down there," I recalled.

Not only was the silence in the golf cart heavy, but it was also tense, as if we were holding our breath, waiting to see what would happen next.

The air was thick with anticipation, and the only sound was the faint hum of the golf cart as Gail started it up and began to move away. Mae, Mama, and I remained motionless, our eyes fixed on Gail's retreating figure. I wondered what secrets and revelations might lie ahead.

Mama kicked her golf cart back in gear, slowly and cautiously driving through the neighborhood, keeping a good distance between us and Gail.

Mama tried to be stealthy, but the sound of the golf cart's engine and the crunch of its tires on the snow on the pavement gave her away. As we passed by, neighbors watched with a mix of curiosity and suspicion, wondering what we were doing while they tried to make snowmen in their front yards.

Mae and I smiled and waved to make the situation seem less creepy, but they continued to watch us as we drove past.

Gail had to have winter tires on her golf cart because she was going so fast, Mama couldn't keep up with her. Once we got on the main road, Gail was nowhere to be found.

Mama proceeded past the houses, including the Strickland compound. I couldn't help but rubberneck to see if I could see any signs of Darren. I'd not yet heard from him today.

"I guess if we can't follow her, we might'swell get in here and see what the Bubbly Boutique has to offer." Mama whipped the golf cart into the parking space along the curb in front of the Jubilee Inn.

CHAPTER NINETEEN

The inside of the boutique was bustling with activity as customers shopped and browsed the various items on display.

"Very festive." Mae pointed out the sparkling lights and decorations adorning the walls and shelves.

"If you've not noticed, the entire village is festive," I told her. "Fern Bank's mama, Nettie, is the owner. So everything in here is top-notch and high dollar, and some are from New York."

Mentioning New York got Mae's attention. She'd lived in the city for a long time and had a great life there. I was very jealous of her big-city style when she came to Normal. She'd lived a dream I'd always seen for myself, but as I'd gotten a little older, I actually cherished the good fortune I'd had and the friendship Mae had given me, despite its rocky start.

"Ooh la la." Servers were circulating the store with trays of sparkling flutes of champagne and offering them to customers. I picked up a glass.

The bubbly drinks added to the festive atmosphere, and from what I saw, customers were sipping on the champagne as they shopped.

Mae, Mama, and I went off in different directions to see what caught our fancy.

The store was filled with the sounds of laughter and conversation as customers chatted with one another and the friendly staff members. I recognized a few people, greeted them with a smile, and told them, "Happy New Year."

I'd not heard anyone mention Hillary Stevens, but I did hear a few murmurs about the Merry Maker and that people were happy to see Cup of Cheer had been chosen for the last hurrah of the year.

The air was filled with the scents of champagne and the excitement of the upcoming New Year's Eve celebration.

From the back corner of the store, the sounds of a fiddler playing lively tunes added to the celebratory mood. As I made my way back to look at the musician, I smiled, watching customers tapping their feet and swaying to the music as they browsed the racks of clothing and accessories.

Overall, the inside of the boutique was festive and lively, with a warm and welcoming atmosphere perfect for ringing in the new year with a little shopping. Something Mae West loved to do.

"Darren?" I didn't mean to say his name out loud but seeing him draw the fiddle bow along the strings with ease and calm put a smile on my face.

His eyes scanned the small group of customers that'd gathered in front of him, me being one of them. Suddenly, his gaze locked onto mine. I felt a surge of energy and emotion wash over me when he smiled with a look of adoration and pride. His fingers flew across the strings of his fiddle with newfound vigor and skill.

As he played, I couldn't keep my eyes off him, and I felt a deep sense of connection and love that seemed to flow between us, which was so electric my eyes filled with tears.

As the song came to an end, he winked and smiled before turning back to the crowd and thanking them for clapping.

"I didn't expect to see you here." Darren dropped the bow and fiddle to his side and took a few steps toward me.

"I can say the same thing," I said and resisted the urge to reach out and touch him. "You really have a talent."

"Thank you. I love playing." He glanced around. "I see your mom and Mae are here."

"Yeah. We thought a little retail therapy would calm our nerves after we went to confront Gail." My words landed a shocked look on his face. "Yep. We decided to go to her house after I found her home address in the *Junction Journal* database."

He snorted a laugh.

"You wouldn't believe it if I described how weird it was because she thought I was there to take her photo for winning the mini-village addition contest." I didn't bother wasting time telling him about Gail getting all gussied up. "When we told her why we were there, she knew we were thinking she was a suspect."

"How did that go?" he asked.

Fern Banks walked up with a tray of champagne and stood there.

"I didn't kill Hillary." She held the tray in the air with one hand and shoved the other on her hip. "Yes, I was drunk, and yes, Darren gave me a warm blanket to sleep, but as far as me going after him or Hillary…" Her head wagged back and forth along her shoulders as her snarky attitude came out of her mouth. "Neither happened."

I opened my mouth to say something.

"Uh-uh." Fern shushed me. "I know what you're going to say."

"No, you don't." I shot back. How dare Fern Banks think she knew me that well.

"Oh, yes, I do. You're going to tell me how me badmouthing Hillary makes it point the finger at me, but just because I say something doesn't mean I'm acting on it. I was blowing off steam, and I have an alibi." She shifted her focus to Darren. "Whether you like it or not. I'm a longtime friend of the Strickland family. It doesn't matter if it's Rhett or Darren. I know I can call on them anytime, and they will help me out. That means if this"—she wagged a finger between Darren and me—"goes anywhere, then you're gonna have to get used to seeing me."

She twisted herself around with the tray as steady as could be, not one flute teetering, as she pranced off in the direction of a group of customers.

"That's that." I shrugged, trying to let the frustration slough off me as if it were that easy. The frustration of not being able to use my investigative skills as a reporter had failed me.

The urgent timing of the situation also left me feeling disappointed and anxiously stressful now that Chief Strickland had given me the thumbs-up to snoop all I could.

"And it doesn't help we have literally no true suspects." I leaned into Darren and whispered, "Mrs. Stevens believes Denise couldn't've done it because they were best friends. Denise was at the ribbon-cutting ceremony. Do you know how mad it makes me that your father gave us the go signal and I can't come up with anything?"

"I stopped looking for my father's approval years ago." Darren looked past me and threw a chin. If not for Mae walking up, I'd have explored his comment a little more. "He called me about Hazelynn saying she made the call about Hillary peeping, but he said he never got a call from Hazelynn."

"Was that what he was doing? Shuffling through the folders looking for the dispatch call?" I wondered why Matthew was looking through the files while we were in his office trying to tell him what we knew.

"Yes. They keep all the backup transcripts and the audio calls. He said he never got a call from Hazelynn, but he did get a call from Berta."

"Berta Bristol." I knew it was her, but saying her name to myself made me remember and recall better for later if I needed to. "Welcome Center Berta?"

"There's no other Berta in Holiday Junction." His voice was tight as he spoke. "What are you thinking?"

"Nothing." I shook my head because I really had no idea what I was thinking. "I wonder if your dad checked out her alibi completely. I mean, things get missed all the time. And I don't want you to step on his toes or anything."

The relationship between Darren and his father was such a slippery slope.

Every time Darren mentioned his family—his father, really—I felt he was opening up a little more and more. That was when I felt the closest to him and thought there was more between us than just this common thread of trying to find the killer or a place to put the Merry Maker sign.

"Like I said, I stopped seeking his approval a long time ago." Nettie called out his name, and he looked over to where she was standing near the counter.

She did a little "air" fiddle motion.

"After I'm done here, I'll give him a call and see what he's got on Berta. But for now, I think it's interesting Hazelynn didn't make the call." The two times he mentioned Hazelynn not calling Matthew like she'd said made my legs feel spongy.

The only other time I'd felt that way was when something deep inside me told me something wasn't right, and I was on the complete wrong path in my journalistic investigations.

"I love your town." Mae tipped back the flute and emptied the contents in her mouth. "That was good. And you are a good fiddler."

"Speaking of that." He drew the fiddle up to his neck and waved the bow in the air. "I had already made the commitment to play today, so we will get together this afternoon and go over some more clues."

"Okay." I smiled. "We are going to do some more shopping before we eat supper at Mama's. But before we head to any other shops, I'd like to stop in Brewing Beans."

"We have to go get a crème brûlée coffee and then walk around. So festive." Mae was enjoying herself, and I was happy to see it.

The competitive side of me made me want to solve Hillary's murder before she went back to Normal. I wasn't about to let her solve murders better than me.

I noticed my old ways and feelings of competition between the two of us creeping back in, only she had no idea I was feeling this way.

"Want to go grab the coffee?" I asked. My eyes glazed over the tops of customers' heads while I scanned the room for Mama.

"Yeah," she agreed. "I think Millie Kay is in the dressing room, if that's who you're trying to find."

"I'll go tell her we are going to grab a coffee, if you want to meet me outside," I told her, and we parted ways.

Carefully navigating through the crowds of people, I tried to avoid bumping into others or knocking over any displays. The clothing racks with the sale signs on them were the most crowded and the closest to the dressing rooms.

I made eye contact with Fern while she continued to strategically maneuver her way around the Bubbly Boutique, but her face didn't look so bubbly. I offered her a sympathetic smile while she tried to steady the tray above her head.

The customers swayed and started to sing the words to "Auld Lang Syne," flutes in the air, while Darren did a great job keeping them on the beat. It was organized chaos that actually made it easier to get to the dressing room.

"Mama?" I called out.

"Back here, honey," she called and wiggled a bare foot underneath the door. "I'm trying on some shoes to go with my outfit."

"You take your time. We are going to Brewing Beans and to walk around a little." I put an ear to the dressing room door when I heard Mama give a little grunt. "Are you okay?"

"These sizes are wrong," she moaned. "I swear they are making clothes smaller and smaller."

I grinned, knowing Mama would soon be going on her annual New Year's diet.

"We will walk home in time for supper," I told her and left her grumbling under her breath about the clothing-size issue.

Once I made it to the door, I turned around and found Darren's eyes were on me. There was a moment between the two of us, a strong sense of affection and adoration that brought me an overwhelming feeling I'd never experienced.

It was so strong, I had to push myself out of the door to stop the feeling.

"Whoa." Mae jerked back. "What is wrong? You nearly knocked me over."

"I, um, I—" I stumbled over the words. My head was all foggy and nothing made sense.

"I know that look." Mae's lips quivered into a smile. "Violet Rhinehammer is in love."

"Stop." I turned on the sidewalk and walked straight to Brewing Beans with my head down so the snowflakes wouldn't smack me in the face. I did my best to ignore her smooching sounds and kissy lips.

"Look at you!" she screamed out loud.

"Stop it." I groaned with gritted teeth when we walked into Brewing Beans. The line was very long. Hazelynn and Hershal were both working alongside a few more employees.

"Hey!" Hazelynn waved her arms, and once she was confident we saw her, she pointed for us to go to the other side of the counter.

The customers' chattering and laughing filled the air, and the hum of the espresso machine mixed with the smell of freshly brewed coffee and sweet pastries curled around me as I made my way over to Hazelynn.

"Mae, I was hoping you'd be in." She'd already had two cups filled and ready for us. "On the house. You gave the best marketing advice and look."

"What on earth did you do?" I asked.

"We were talking about social media, and I called Gert Hobson to see if she could give me some quick social tips." Mae acted like it was no big deal. "I'm glad to see it worked."

"Violet, you've got a good one here." Hazelynn pointed at Mae. "Too bad we can't keep her here because she said she was leaving on the first."

"I've only got a few months to plan a wedding, and I promised my fiancé I'd start on the first." Mae wagged the emerald ring in the air. "If things go right, I might be back here for a wedding."

"Who is getting married?" Hazelynn's eyes grew. "We love weddings around here."

"You love any day you can celebrate." I kicked Mae in the shin with my foot.

145

"Ouch," she yelped and bent down to rub the little nudge out. She shot me a look, and I gave it back to her. "Fine."

"Any news on the case?" Hazelynn talked to Mae like they'd had a conversation I'd not been privy to.

"We are still trying to come up with a list of suspects." Mae took a sip.

"You get here really early." I held the cup in both hands. "Are you sure you don't recall seeing anyone?"

"Like I told you, Troy and I were standing here when Hillary started that peeping Tom stuff. That was when I called the Chief. He never showed." Hazelynn was very convincing she'd called.

"Are you sure you called?" I asked.

"I can show you." She reached for her cell phone and started to go through the call history feature. Her body tensed as she shifted her weight to one side. She hit the screen of her phone a few more times, looking as though she was trying to piece together something she was certain she'd done.

"I have no idea why it's not in here." She wagged her phone. "I can't seem to find it, but I know." Her jaw dropped. "You know, Berta Bristol had come in as soon as I started to dial Matthew's number, and she told me she'd just called Matthew. That was why I didn't call him."

"Berta?" I made sure I heard her correctly. "You and Troy were in here and saw Hillary. You went to call Matthew, but Berta showed up, and she'd already called him?"

"Yeah, she said she ran into Hillary right before she got here, and Hillary was going nuts about the mini-village, shoved Berta, and took off." Hazelynn pointed at her elbow. "Berta had a nasty scratch on her arm. I asked her if Hillary did it, and she said no, one of the displays for the mini-village had some sort of pottery tool, and when she was placing all the additions in the village, she scraped herself."

"Pottery tool?" Mae grabbed on to the edge of the counter as though she'd just lost her balance.

"Yeah. Troy and I were standing right here. I'd just brewed the first batch of crème brûlée for the season because he took the first batch to his mom. We were waiting for it to finish brewing, and that was when all of this happened." Hazelynn signed, "I told you Denise loved it. Did the coffee box not work that day?"

"No, it did. Berta never mentioned coming here that morning." I got a funny feeling in my stomach. "Matthew never showed up here after Berta called him?"

"He didn't. But I guess I didn't call him." She sighed, trying to recall again, as if she was sure she'd done it. "I swear my memory isn't what it used to be. After Berta was all flustered, it was time to open the shop, so after that, I was busy."

Mae grabbed her coat.

"Are you thinking what I'm thinking?" she asked. Both of us had dismissed the idea that Berta was the murderer.

An intense focus and determination grew on Mae's face, as if we were both trying to analyze the clues we had and piece them together in this tidy little murder's puzzle.

"Yeah." I nodded once the clues started to fit rather nicely. "Hazelynn, thanks. You've been a big help."

Instantly, I knew we had to go back to the Welcome Center. The murder weapon was in the mini-village this entire time. Staring at me in the face. Taunting me.

CHAPTER TWENTY

M ae West and I tripped all over each other making our way to the Welcome Center. At least the snow had stopped falling, but the temperature was still frigid.

"Berta Bristol has to be the killer." I wanted to work out all the clues with Mae before we got to the Welcome Center to confront Berta.

"I'm listening." Mae's hands were tucked inside the pockets of her coat.

As our feet struck the pavement, the fresh layer of snow packed down, making a loud crunch on the layer of thin ice below.

"Berta takes pride in the Welcome Center. It's her job. Prudence told us that Berta came into the tea shop and gave the Stevenses ample warning about Hillary." I kept my eyes focused on the journey to the Welcome Center instead of watching people putting the finishing touches on the midnight celebration at Holiday Fountain as we hurried past.

"She also said Berta warned them if they didn't keep Hillary away, she'd have to take matters into her own hands," Mae recalled, her chin nearly touching her chest as if she were trying to keep her face out of the whipping cold wind.

"Plus she's on the Village Council, where Hillary went to protest a lot of things," I said through my chattering teeth. "The mini-village is the only thing keeping tourists coming to the Welcome Center, and if it's gone, Berta's job is gone. The only way the mini-village would be gone was if there were no mini-village."

The silence between Mae and me the last few hundred feet we walked to the Welcome Center was almost as loud and unnerving as the confrontation we were anticipating with Berta.

Mae took her hand out of her pocket and touched me when we got to the Welcome Center.

"I will record the conversation. You make sure you've got 911 pulled up in case she tries something funny." Mae had a good plan of action. "We want to make sure we see the New Year."

"We want to make sure you get married." I smiled and led her into the building.

The building was packed with tourists who were enjoying the mini-village. Most of them had a ballot in their hands to vote for the newest addition. The winner would be announced at the stroke of midnight tomorrow on New Year's Eve. Then the town would make their way to Cup of Cheer, where the Merry Maker had decided the final party of the year would be.

As the Merry Maker, I was determined to make sure Holiday Junction started the new year off with Hillary's killer behind bars.

"Do you see her?" Mae asked me.

I curled up on my toes and scanned the crowd, turning my head left and right in search of Berta.

"Over there." I started to push my way through the crowd after I'd spotted her. I moved quickly as possible so she wouldn't be able to disappear on me.

"Mae?" I called out behind me and glanced a little farther back. The line I'd forged to get to Berta had closed with tourists between her and me.

She flung her hand toward me, indicating that I should go on and she'd catch up.

"Crud," I groaned when I got to the spot where I'd seen Berta before I'd made my way over there. She was gone.

I looked around and got a glimpse of her from the back. She was walking down the hall where the offices were.

I held my hand above the crowd and pointed at the hallway when Mae's eyes caught mine. After she nodded at me and knew she'd seen me, I darted off after Berta.

"Violet." Berta heard me come into the room and jumped around. She was bent over a desk looking for something. Her shirt sleeve was pulled up over her elbow, and some blood—both frank and fresh—was pooled up on her arm. "You scared me."

"Let's talk about your arm." I wanted to keep her scared. Even though Mae wasn't in there yet to record the conversation during which I would get Berta to confess, I started to question her, hoping Mae would arrive soon.

"It's fine. I don't think it needs stitches." She had gotten a tissue off her desk and started to blot at her arm. "I have been using Band-Aids. But if it keeps up, I'll just run over to the hospital."

She was good. Very calm for a killer. Even her body language was hard for me to read.

"Hillary isn't fine. She can't just run across the street to the hospital," I blurted out.

A wave of questions, like it was a silly statement I'd made, landed on her face.

"Are you accusing me of killing Hillary Stevens?" she asked.

I snorted, tipping my head back a little.

"Are you telling me you didn't have motive?" I started to rattle off all the reasons why she would kill Hillary. "After all, with Hillary out of the way you don't have to worry about the mini-village being destroyed, which is why you are on the Village Council. If there's no display here, they won't need your input on the council. Nor will they need to pay you because, after all, the only other things here are the brochures for all the shops and stores in the village—and bathrooms. And I'm guessing you don't want to be a janitor."

"Is this some sort of joke?" Berta reached for the phone on her desk. "Maybe Chief Strickland can sort this out."

"You mean like you killed Hillary here with the new addition of the awl in the mini-village. You stabbed her in the side and killed her before you dragged her body over to the castle because let's face it..." I assessed that I could probably take her out if she tried something on me, so I stalked over to her. "Only you know where all the mini-village pieces go, and if someone else killed Hillary, then they left a messy trail of small pieces."

Berta nervously fussed with her hands, which she clasped and dropped to her belly.

"I think I'm going to be sick." She doubled over.

"You aren't going to get out of this one. My friend Mae is out there right now calling Chief Strickland." I pointed back at the door, which Mae had not yet come through. I quickly dismissed the thoughts of where she had possibly gone. She knew I was in here with the killer.

Berta's body began to physically shake, and her throat started to heave.

"Berta?" I placed a hand on her back. "Are you okay?"

"No." She felt behind her for the chair, and I helped ease her down.

"You killed Hillary Stevens. You told her parents if they didn't keep her from the mini-village, then you'd take matters into your own hands." I didn't tell her that Prudence was the one who'd given me the information.

Literal sobs left her body, her head in her hands.

"Do you want me to call Chief Strickland? Or do you want me to escort you over to the police department?" I was giving her the option so as not to make a scene in the Welcome Center if the police came in.

It was also easy enough to walk her across the street to the police department. Otherwise, I would have already called Matthew to pick her up.

"I didn't do it." She looked up. Her eyes were already red and puffy. "But I know who did," she said through a congested nose.

"Who?" Confused, I shook my head.

"Violet," Mae called from behind me.

Before I could look back at her, I felt a slight jab in my side.

I jerked away from the pain, and when I did, I came face-to-face with the killer.

Troy Kenner.

CHAPTER TWENTY-ONE

"If you'd only kept your nose out of it." Troy had Mae, Berta, and me backed into the corner of Berta's office. "This is going to get a little messy."

He waved an awl in his hand. My mind darted back and forth, imagining scenarios of the physically strongest of the three women kicking the awl out of Troy's hand while one of the others jumped on him and took him down while the third called for help.

"We should've known it was you." Mae nudged me. "Tell him, Violet."

"I, um..." My vision blurred, and my mouth dried.

"Violet," Mae urged through her gritted teeth. "Tell him."

"I should've known when I saw you running out of Brewing Beans, stopping me from calling Chief Strickland on her." Tears ran down Berta's face as she told the truth of what had taken place that morning. "I didn't even think of it until just now when she accused me of killing Hillary."

"Stop talking," he warned her and pointed the awl at her.

"We need the truth. I'm going to tell it before I die!" she screamed at him. "I got my coffee, and on my way back to the Welcome Center, I started to get nervous and that was when I called Chief Strickland and

153

got the dispatch. When they answered, I told them never mind because the Welcome Center looked fine. I went into my office and didn't even notice Hillary's body had been added by you.

"When Darren and I asked you about Hillary, you left out the part where you'd gone to Brewing Beans and gotten the first crème brûlée. Hillary didn't come there to be a peeping Tom. She knew you were going to be there, so she was looking for you."

It was all coming together.

"She wanted you to go with her to the village and mess up a few things, but you decided to change your mind. You were able to stop Berta from calling on her while you went to talk to her." I told my theory and kept an eye on the awl in his hand, trying to anticipate his next move or even give time for someone to jump him.

"She was already moving things around, and you confronted her about it." I wasn't really sure how things went, but I could guess by the look on his face that I was pretty darn close.

"You tried to talk to her, and she wasn't listening. She was going to destroy everything your mother worked for, which was the one thing that you inherited. Ceramic Celebration." I hit the nail on the head.

"You realized Hillary's ways of dealing with change weren't going to do anything. She didn't even listen to you." Mae found her voice and spoke up, leaving Berta alone and crying in the corner.

Mae took a step up next to me. Her confidence fueled me even more than I'd already fueled myself.

"She didn't even see it coming." My eyes narrowed in on his. "You took the awl Gail Steinner had used in her design for the flagpole on top of the castle. You used your dominant hand, with the pointed end of the awl facing forward. Then you approached Hillary from the side, positioning yourself so that her body was in between you and the awl. Then you raised your arm and aimed the pointed end of the awl toward Hillary's side."

"You targeted the abdomen," Mae said, the words seething out of her gritted teeth. "With a quick, forceful motion, you thrust the awl into

Hillary's body, pushing it all the way through until the pointed end caught something inside and she slumped over in pain."

"It wasn't until after you realized what you'd done that you knew you needed to push off her murder on someone else because after all the work you'd done to do exactly what your mother wanted, you weren't going to go to jail. But you knew you would be the hero if you got rid of the village nuisance." My words must have struck a chord with him since his emotions started to show on the outside. "You know how to make a good knot because you have a boat. That was the knot you made with Hillary's hair to tie her up to the castle."

He clenched his jaw and tried hard to fight back the tears.

"Hillary was my friend. I had to stop her pain." He acted like he'd done her a favor. "She couldn't stop herself. It was like an addiction, the attention she got, and she wanted me to help her. I told her it was time for her to grow up and see the world for what it was. But she couldn't!"

The office door burst open.

"Hold it right there, Troy." Chief Matthew Strickland stood with his gun pointed at Troy. "Hazelynn recalled you'd told her you'd call me and you didn't. You came here to take care of Hillary because the statement Berta gave me after the murder coincided with Hazelynn's recollection, giving you a very good timeline to have come here and killed Hillary Stevens."

Troy didn't budge. He kept staring at me with the awl in his hand.

"Drop the awl and turn around." Matthew kept his calm while my insides were screaming to leave my body. I didn't dare move a muscle.

The awl hit the office floor with a thud.

"Troy Kenner, you are under arrest for the murder of Hillary Stevens." Matthew unclipped the handcuffs from his belt and took a step forward to take Troy into custody.

A few more deputies filed in and took over, taking Mae, Berta, and me to a different room of the Welcome Center to get our statements.

I sat at a conference table facing the window. The backdrop consisted of the mountains behind the Welcome Center. I noticed Matthew had taken Troy out of the back of the building to put him into the cruiser. A good move, one that wouldn't let on to the tourists what was really happening.

"Please tell my friend Mae that I'll be out front waiting for her after she gives her statement," I told the officer, since they'd kept us apart.

When I walked out of the hallway, I was at ease. Not nervous or upset. I was happy this case was solved and even happier I was alive.

My eyes slowly shifted to look at the castle where Troy had tied Hillary by her own long hair, and I smiled when I saw the awl Gail Steinner had used in her piece as a flagpole was missing. The police had taken it off because it was in fact the murder weapon Troy had cleaned and put back on the castle. The weapon was hidden in plain sight, but it also pointed at Gail as the killer.

I shook my head and gave a deep sigh of relief as I made my way past all the tourists and waited for Mae, my heart grateful that Hillary would finally have peace.

CHAPTER TWENTY-TWO

"**A**re you two ready?" The next afternoon, almost twenty-four hours to the time Mae and I were held at awl-point, Mama stood at my door.

She wore her red coat with the black fur lining and matching gloves. The mirror ball earrings twirled from her earlobes, having their own little dance party.

"It's time." She smiled when she saw Mae and I had on the gold lamé jumpsuits she'd gotten for us. "We don't want to miss out on the Merry Maker drop."

"Do you think we can stop by Brewing Beans after?" Mae had really taken to the local coffee shop. "I'll be leaving soon, and I want to get a bag of coffee beans to take back to Gert Hobson."

"How is Gert?" I quickly checked the online paper and made sure it had posted about both the Merry Maker final party and the festive activities going on all day to celebrate the last day of the year.

"She's great. Busy as ever." Mae checked her image in the mirror on the wall before she put her coat on over her lamé outfit. "Millie Kay, I wasn't sure this outfit was going to fit since I was so full of last night's supper. There's nothing like a good home-cooked meal after a long day of catching a killer."

"Now you be sure to tell Mary Elizabeth I made her biscuits from the Normal Baptist Church cookbook we put together when we were in the bell choir." Mama knew Mary Elizabeth would get a kick out of that. "And before I forget, you tell her to come back with you next time."

"She'd love that." Mae didn't tell Mama or even say anything to me about Darren stopping over in the middle of the night.

I wasn't even sure if Mae had heard him or if her moving around in the attic was her simply tossing and turning.

Nothing had taken place other than Darren coming over to make sure I was okay after what he'd heard about Troy cornering us. Darren told me he'd gone to the station to talk to Troy.

Troy had told Darren he regretted it but felt like Hillary would've done something so drastic he somehow had justified the murder as giving her real peace from her inner demons.

Mama didn't mention that he'd come over, either, even though she'd flipped on the floodlights in back of the house. That was her way of letting me know without letting me know she knew he was there.

"Come on. I've got the golf cart all warmed up." Mama wasn't about to let us walk to Holiday Fountain, even though the temperature had warmed up to over fifty degrees.

Since we'd not left the house all day and stayed in to catch up on all the gossip from Normal, the sun had made its way out during the day and melted away a lot of the snow.

"Promise me you're coming home for my wedding." Mae seemed more confident than ever about getting back to plan the wedding of a lifetime. At least one of the residents of Normal was going to think they were like the royal couple.

"I promise." After I put my coat on, I crisscrossed my finger on the front of my coat across my chest. I grabbed the camera I'd gotten for the *Junction Journal* so I could take photos for tomorrow's online article. "Maybe I'll have a plus-one."

"You better bring that cutie." She winked and waited for me to lock the door before we headed through the backyard and out the squeaky gate. "After tonight, I must get back to check in with my new sister-in-law to be."

"Good luck with that one." I snorted, knowing just how much of a handful Ellis Sharp would be, especially now that she'd called and told Mae that her parents had cut her off financially. "I'd not wish Ellis Sharp on my worst enemy."

"Not even Fern Banks?" Mae's snarky joke fell flat on me as we got into the golf cart. "Joking. Lighten up, Violet." Mae grabbed the zipper and zipped up the plastic golf cart enclosure so Mama could take off.

The town square was decorated with sparkling lights and colorful streamers. A large banner said Happy New Year in bold letters.

Large balloons in the shape of numbers representing the new year were tied down to the amphitheater set up for live music and performances, with speakers and microphones for announcements.

Food and drink stands offering a variety of festive treats and beverages had long lines with eager tourists ready to ring in the new year.

People dancing, chatting, and enjoying the celebration made for perfect photo footage for the paper.

"This is the Sparkle Ball?" Mae must've thought the ball took place in an actual ballroom.

"Yep." I winked and let the camera dangle from the strap around my neck so I could grab two flutes of champagne from the tray of the woman walking by.

The atmosphere came alive when the DJ took over the sound system, getting people on the dance floor in front of the amphitheater.

"Thank goodness the Village Council shot your mama down about the Leading Ladies doing a little number," Mae said with a snort.

"Cheers to that!" I had to holler over the music as we clinked glasses.

"Hey, you!" Darren's hot breath tickled the back of my neck when he saddled up behind me.

I whipped around, and he had on a pair of glasses with rims in the shape of the upcoming year.

"Happy New Year, Mae." He smiled.

My emotions were all over the board from excitement to anticipation with butterflies in my stomach, making my heart race.

"Happy New Year." Her eyes moved between Darren and me. "Did you see the photo booth over there?"

"I did." Darren gave her the side-eye but kept his attention on me.

"Why don't you two go get a photo?" She shrugged. "I'm going to go say my goodbyes to some of the locals I met."

She walked away, leaving Darren and me alone.

"I think she has a great idea." He took my flute from me and set them both down on one of the stationary tray before he took my hand and guided me over to one of the photo booths.

"I've always wanted to do one of these," I said nervously and glanced down at the small bench, which was only big enough for two small people. Not a big man like him and a small woman like me.

He slid the coins in the slot, and the change *clinked* when it hit the bottom. Then he pulled the curtain to close us inside.

"I've been wanting to do this." He sat down and pulled me on his lap.

My long hair threaded around his fingers as he placed his hand on the back of my head, drawing me closer to him. A vague, sensuous light passed between us before our lips met.

My heart jolted and my pulse pounded.

The click of the flashbulb from the photo booth made me jump back. We both laughed, looked at the camera box, and smiled just as it took another photo.

"I'm not sure what it is about you, but I think we need to give this a go." Every time he looked at me, my heart flipped.

"Us?" I swallowed hard.

"Yes. Us." He peered at me intently. The sound of the finished photos clinked in the photo slot.

He reached around me, took the strip of three tiny photos, and showed them to me with a grin.

"We look great together." He held it out for me to see. "Especially the one that caught us doing this."

He leaned in again and gave me a soft, warm kiss that lingered for a few seconds before the curtains ripped open.

"It's about darn time." Mama stood there with her hands on her hips. "Now you two get out here and show the world you're meant to be together."

"Yes, ma'am." Darren stood up and cradled me in his arms. He took me with him all the way to the fountain, where the Merry Maker outline was about to start its descent to ring in the new year.

"Five, four, three, two," I hollered with the rest of the crowd but kept my eye on Darren, who was also staring back at me. "One!"

"Happy New Year, Violet Rhinehammer," Darren whispered, taking me into his arms and giving me a New Year's kiss to remember.

CHAPTER TWENTY-THREE

As New Year's Day wore on, Mama had fixed the Southern New Year's Day lunch before Mae had to get on an airplane back to Normal.

Mama had even invited Darren over so he'd learn the traditional feast of black-eyed peas, cornbread, beans, and collard greens.

My heart was in two different places, playing tug-of-war with my emotions. I was excited to explore the new relationship with Darren and sad to see Mae leave.

The sun was setting on our golf cart ride to the airport. Mama had stayed behind so Mae and I could spend a few minutes alone before she left.

A warm glow emanated over the mountains. The shadows stretched out across the landscape, and the trees were painted in golden light. The air was still and quiet, as if the whole world was holding its breath in awe of the beauty around it on this first day of the new year.

"It'll be late when you get home," I said. "I'm sorry we have very limited flights out."

"I don't mind. I love seeing that." She pointed out the mountain as the sun dipped below the horizon, and the stars began to twinkle in the sky. The moon had started to rise, casting a soft, silvery glow over Holiday Junction.

It was a moment to savor and treasure.

"Your town is showing off for me." She winked and unzipped the plastic around the golf cart, which I'd brought to a stop.

We both got out, and I walked with her into the airport. There wasn't any need for all the security the big-city airports had. I was able to walk her right up to the gate, past Dave, and the TSA agent.

Rhett had met us at the door leading to the outside, where Mae would walk up the ladder to board the small jet.

"Tell everyone back home that I'm doing awesome. I'm amazing and the best reporter out here," I teased, just a smidgen, as I watched her walk up the metal steps and enter the small airplane.

I stood on the tarmac at the small airport with Rhett and Dave next to me. Mae's face took up the entire small port airplane window as she waved out to us.

The smile on her face brought me warm memories of home and what she'd be going back to. Those feelings didn't override the feelings the hopes the new year had put inside of me.

"So, what's the truth about you and my cousin?" Rhett asked me as we turned and went back into the small airport. Dave clucked along right next to us.

"He's turned out to be a good friend." I wasn't a kiss-and-tell type.

"I sure wished I'd outbid him on that lighthouse," he muttered.

I jerked my head and looked at him. No wonder Darren was so bent on buying it. There was so much history between the two that didn't stop at the competition from when they were younger. It'd obviously spilled over into their adulthood.

I appreciated that Darren felt like he could confide in me at his parents' house the night they'd had my family, Mae, and me over for supper. But one thing stuck out from all of that confessing. The *if I stick around* part.

True, Holiday Junction was never on my list of places to visit in my lifetime. I'd never even heard of the place until the plane made the emergency landing. My adventure that day was to further my career, no matter who I'd left behind.

I had to admit my plan this entire time had not been to stay here, but the more time I spent here and got ingrained in the holiday traditions, the more I felt part of the community.

I wasn't sure what the new year had in store for me, but one thing I did know was that Holiday Junction felt like home more than my hometown ever did.

For now, I was staying put. At least the rest of this year.

After all, I was the Merry Maker, and I had plans.

CHAPTER TWENTY-FOUR

Note from the Merry Maker

Cheers to a new year and another chance for us to get it right. As the Merry Maker, I was delighted to see all the tourists and citizens of Holiday Junction gather at Cup of Cheer last night after the image of me dropped into the new year.

So many faces with hopeful and optimistic looks for what the future could hold. Excitement and anticipation about the opportunities and challenges lying ahead were felt.

Think of all the good teaching Gail Steinner is giving to all the children and their families. Holiday Junction sure could use many more citizens like Gail.

Speaking of doing good, we would be remiss if we didn't talk about Hillary Stevens, who only wanted to do good by the community by keeping her fond memories alive. After all, it was her big heart that loved our village so much she didn't want it to change.

Is it just me, or did Chief Strickland solve this one fast—so fast it makes you wonder if he only did it because we are now into a new election year, and let's just say he's due for a little competition?

But that's not for me to decide. Though I can't help but wonder if the light in the lighthouse will shine some light on the Stricklands.

Only the new year will tell. Overall, I hope the new year will bring a sense of optimism, positivity, and determination for us all, but I wouldn't count on it.

For now, Happy New Year.

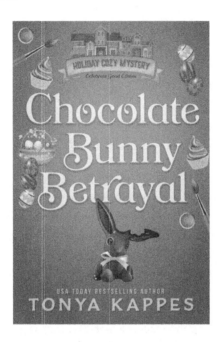

Keep reading for a sneak peek of the next book in the series. Chocolate Bunny Betrayal is now available to purchase on Amazon or read for FREE in Kindle Unlimited.

Chapter One of Book Five
Chocolate Bunny Betrayal

"This is all wrong." Mama scraped the side of the big pot that sat atop one of the many stoves in the Incubator, a kitchen that amateur chefs and bakers used in the back of the Freedom Diner.

"You didn't put enough water in the boiler." Nate Lustig, the diner's owner and the head honcho of the Incubator, stood over Mama's shoulder, giving her pointers. "See?" He lifted the double boiler and had Mama look inside. "All gone. Evaporated!"

He clapped, making her jump.

"We can fix it." Nate grabbed a few ingredients and some heavy cream. He poured them in while Mama vigorously stirred.

I was too busy with my own dark chocolate concoction to worry about what Mama was doing. The small bunny molds would be perfect for the dark chocolate treats I'd planned to give out to the friends I'd made in Holiday Junction while working at the Easter-egg-dyeing station for the Hip Hop Hurray Easter Festival.

It was my first Easter here, and with the huge town Bake-Off to celebrate the holiday, I'd agreed to come with Mama to the Incubator. She'd entered the Bake-Off and could perfect her Easter dirt cake here. She claimed the chocolate bunnies she was going to outline the cake with would make her the winner, which was why she insisted on getting the melted chocolate just right.

The sound of the aerosol can of cooking spray I was using to coat the bunny molds combined with the whirring of mixers and a blender, the clanging of pots and pans, the sizzling of pans on the stove, and the clinking of utensils other people used.

Nate moved around the kitchen and gave the occasional shout or conversation between himself and one of the bakers. Though this was his weekly baking class, most of the bakers in the Incubator were also contestants in the big Bake-Off.

When I heard the squeak of the oven doors opening and closing and the beeping of timers going off, I looked around to see who had either started or ended the baking process.

Frances Green had called Nate over to test the cake she'd taken out of the oven. She was one of Mama's toughest competitors.

Nate's fork slid through the slice of chocolate cake. He put it in his mouth and raked the tines along the bottoms of his teeth as a look of pure bliss forced his eyes to close.

It was almost like I could also savor the rich chocolate that made Nate's lips curl up into a satisfied smile.

"Perfect," Nate said. He let out a small sigh of contentment and then took another bite of the moist, fluffy cake.

Frances clapped in delight. The lines around her mouth deepened as her smile grew. She pushed back a few of the loose strands of grey hair that'd fallen out of her topknot and straightened her shoulders as her inner confident baker came out. It was no secret that Frances had won the Bake-Off last year and was here with a passion to win again, making the competition fierce.

Well, for Mama at least. And when I caught Mama looking at Frances, I saw a fire in Mama's eyes, one I'd seen before. The kind of spark that gave her a challenge, and that was what she lived for.

Frances reached around her waist and untied her apron before she tossed it into the dirty hamper.

"The perfect balance of sweetness and chocolate in every bite." Nate bit into the treat again as if he needed to back up his statement. "Every bite."

"Thank you." Frances slid her gaze over to Mama with a wry smile. "This isn't even the recipe I'm going to enter into the contest."

"By the smile on your face, you look like you've got someone special." Willow Johnson pulled her shoulders up to her ears as she blushed.

"I do," Frances whispered loudly enough for me to make out the words that piqued my interest. "But I can't tell anyone. Yet."

"Good for you." Willow conveyed her excitement in a touch above a hushed tone. "You deserve it. Especially after all the time you put into Holiday Junction."

I turned my body slightly so I could hear them a little better, but I wasn't quick enough.

Frances's phone alarm sounded. She took the phone out of her apron pocket.

"I'll be back later to make the one for the competition. I'm going to be late for the audition if I don't get out of here now." Frances's smile never faltered from when Willow asked about the special someone.

In fact, Frances's smile got bigger as she walked closer to Mama.

"I see you made some hollow chocolate bunnies. I bet they are so good." Frances looked over Mama's shoulder. "I love a good chocolate bunny."

Frances pointed at the ten molds Mama had made to surround her cake with the first time around.

"Would you like one?" Mama asked.

"I'd love one. Thank you, Millie Kay." Frances scanned down the line, trying to decide which bunny looked appetizing to her. "How did you know chocolate bunnies are my favorite?"

"Just a guess. I have one special just for you." Mama bent down and took one out of the baking case she'd brought from home.

"It has eyes and a little button candy nose." Frances took the one Mama had made at home for practice. Mama had even put pastel sugar candy buttons on the chocolate bunny for more detail for the nose, eyes, and teeth. "These are adorable."

"Thank you." Mama was proud of what she'd done at home, but today she couldn't even melt the chocolate properly, much less make any sort of bunnies to go around her cake.

"I'll eat this while I go judge the annual bunny competition. I can guarantee there are going to be some big changes, and some people aren't going to like them." Frances waved the chocolate bunny in the air on her way out the door. "You better hurry up."

"Mama, that was nice of you." I wanted her to know I was proud of her, since she'd been yammering on and on about Frances being tough competition for her.

"Ahem." Mama intentionally cleared her throat to make me look at her. It was her way of telling me she didn't want me to mention the kind gesture again unless it was necessary. "We'll have to come back. I have to be at the Easter Bunny auditions in about five minutes, and you have to take the photos," she said, reminding me of the article I was doing for the *Junction Journal*.

I glanced up at the clock on the wall to check the time. The past few hours had gone by fast, and I'd yet to get my mold into the refrigerator.

"Oh no," Willow Johnson cried out over the hum of her mixer. "It's already time for the audition?"

She flipped the switch and ran her fingers down the front of her apron, leaving a chocolate streak trail before she used the apron's bottom edges to wipe her hands down.

"Maximus is probably wondering where I'm at." She untied her apron, wadded it up, and placed it on the mixer. When she hurried off, it fell to the ground. "I'll be back," she called over her shoulder and ran out of the building.

"Then we have to hurry," I told her, starting to scoop my melted dark chocolate out of the pan and into the molds. "Nate," I called to him.

He looked up.

"Can I leave these in the freezer until later?" I asked. "We have to get to the bunny auditions."

I wasn't a judge like Mama. She was a new member on the Village Council and had the hard task of choosing the perfect bunny for the village's Hip Hop Hurray event.

"I'm going to start fresh later." Mama literally tossed everything, including the top pan of the double boiler, in the large jute sack she'd used to bring all her ingredients in from home. "Are you ready?" Mama gave me the side eye.

"Let me get these into the refrigerator and snap a few quick photos."

Carefully, I picked up each mold, walked them across the test kitchen, and placed them on a shelf in the walk-in freezer.

"Violet! Let's go!" Mama had already left the Incubator and stood outside on the sidewalk, yelling for me, swinging her baking box back and forth.

"Thanks, Nate." I offered a wry smile in an attempt to apologize for Mama's behavior. At times like these, she wasn't so southern and lady-like as she thought she was.

"I think I've lost my touch," Mama whined before she picked up her speed, swinging her arms.

The weather was warm and sunny, with clear blue skies and a gentle breeze coming off the ocean. It was nice to see the beach crowded with people who had come to Holiday Junction to enjoy the holiday.

Mama stomped down the seaside sidewalk on the way toward the lighthouse. We were trying to catch the trail leading up to Holiday Park, where the main events of the Hip Hop Hurray Festival would take place.

It was best not to say anything to her or answer her when she was like this, which I'd learned a long time ago.

Instead of commenting, I grunted a few *mm-hhmm*s and did a little window shopping. It was fun to see how the small shops along the seashore had decorated their display windows. Easter-themed decorations such as bunnies, eggs, and pastel colors seemed to be the décor of choice.

A few children darted around Mama then around me as their parents called for them, but the excitement of holiday chocolate was smeared all over their faces.

I sucked in a deep breath, taking in the scent of saltwater mixed with sunscreen that filled the air. The sound of waves crashing on the shore was so soothing and made me smile.

I'd really fallen in love with Holiday Junction without even knowing it.

One big cardboard Easter Bunny was duct-taped to the black door of the jiggle joint. No doubt Darren Strickland had gone to such great efforts to fulfil the Village Council's request that all businesses in Holiday Junction put out some sort of decoration for the holiday.

It took all my willpower not to open the door and slip in where Darren Strickland was working on this week's liquor order.

"Violet Rhinehammer!" Mama stopped, turned around, threw her hands on her hips, and glared. "What are you doing? Stop lollygagging this instant," she snapped and twirled back around, walking like one of those speed walkers at the mall.

I gave one last look at the bar's door and sighed. Seeing Darren would have to wait.

"Violet!" Mama yelled her one-last-time-or-she-would-scold-me yell, even though I was almost thirty years old. "The Leisure Center will be a great place for the Leading Ladies to practice, and I found the perfect place."

"You found a place?" She got my attention, because that was a sure sign the idea had formed into a more solid planning stage.

I hurried up beside her with full attention.

"Did you hear me about the Leisure Center?" Mama had this crazy idea that Holiday Junction needed a place for seniors to go. "I'm telling you I'd be really good at helping people my age."

"Your age?" I questioned. "You're sixty."

Mama had gotten a harebrained idea that Holiday Junction needed something like a senior center, only she named it the Leisure Center. She'd been eyeballing a few older buildings in the area, and it seemed like she'd settled on one.

"We won't have to practice outside in all the elements anymore," she said and hurried up the sidewalk leading from the seaside to Holiday Park.

The sun shone brightly on this beautiful spring day as the Hip Hop Hurray Easter Festival was being set up in the large park.

The park was bustling. Vendors were setting up their booths on the far side of the park, toward the bubbling fountain. The echo from the Leading Ladies inside the bowl of the amphitheater filled the air, as did the laughter of tourists who came off the lake as they paddled around in the large swan boats.

Spring was one of my favorite seasons, and since this was my first spring here, Holiday Junction didn't disappoint.

"I'll be over in a few!" Mama yelled at the Leading Ladies to let them know her itinerary.

Few.

"Isn't it gorgeous here?" Mama must've felt the light in her spirit too. "After a long winter, I'm so glad to have this sunshine." She tucked her arm in my elbow and pointed out what the committee had done to make this year's Hip Hop Hurray Easter Festival the best yet.

And that included her participation in the Leading Ladies production as well as taking home the Golden Egg Trophy for winning the stiff baking competition.

The park was adorned with colorful decorations and flowers hanging from baskets suspended from the planters on the carriage lights. The banners hanging from the dowel rods fluttered in the breeze, adding to the festive atmosphere. The large fountain in the park's center was a popular spot, with children running around and splashing in the cool water.

It was funny to see seven Easter Bunnies all lined up near a banquet table in various types of outfits, trying to win the coveted title to play the Easter Bunny during the entire Hip Hop Hurray Easter Festival. They took that very seriously around here.

"Don't forget to get me sitting at the judges' table," Mama told me as she ran her hand over her shoulder-length blond hair with a hint of gray around the scalp. Her makeup was as perfect as if she'd just left the makeup counter at a high-end department store.

Mama was every part of the southern lady she had always been, even though we no longer lived in the South.

"How do I look?" She tugged at the hem of her monogrammed three-quarter-length sweater as it lay against her jeans.

"You look fantastic," I told her. "And you'll be the prettiest picture I take all day."

Mama hurried over to the judges' table and sat in the chair on the far right, leaving a chair open between her and Emily, the owner of Emily's Treasures. Frances hadn't taken her middle seat at the judges' table. I took the moment to snap a few shots of Mama sitting there so Frances wouldn't be in the photos. Or at least I wouldn't have to crop them out if Mama was standing over my shoulder at the office while I wrote the article.

I moseyed around, slipping in and out of the crowd milling around the park to get some action shots for the *Junction Journal*.

There were six bunnies in costume, and they were all completely different. They were also carrying baskets filled to the brim with colored eggs. Some looked to be the real dyed kind, making me shiver, since I'd done my civic duty as a member of the village and volunteered for a couple of hours during the festival at the egg-dyeing table. The other baskets looked like they were filled with plastic eggs. But the one bunny basket that really got my attention was the one with the two little baby bunnies nestled inside.

"Easter Bunny," I said as I approached and wiggled my camera in the air, "may I take your photo for the *Junction Journal?*"

The bunny nodded and then turned slightly, gave the little cotton tail a little wiggle, and came my way with a little hopping action.

Before too long, the four other bunnies had hopped over, trying to get me to take a photo.

They had really gotten their ability to grab a child's attention down —and my attention too.

One hopped around in a playful manner, attempting to catch my eye by playing peek-a-boo. Another had started to clap the paws and give a little squeal while waving at me.

But the one who rattled a plastic egg, indicating that something was inside, and then offered it to me really got my attention.

"I'm a sucker for Easter candy," I teased and snapped a few photos that included all the bunnies before they hopped away.

I sure didn't envy Mama, Emily, and Frances's job. They were going to have a hard time picking which one would be the best because they all looked great to me.

All but the fifth one, who wore a distinctive bow tie and had not tried to come over but was hopping toward the judges' table.

"Smart," I whispered and brought the camera up to my eye, using my hand to manually zoom in.

In the bliss of watching the bunny stand behind Mama and tease her by trying to take her baking box, I didn't even see Darren Strickland come up behind me.

"Looks like someone is trying to win over Millie Kay." His deep voice and warm breath on my ear made me jump.

"You scared me, Darren Strickland." I playfully smacked him on the arm. "I see the Mad Fiddlers are setting up after the Leading Ladies rehearse."

"I think the Merry Maker picked an *egg*-cellent spot this year." Darren made a horrible joke.

As the editor, photographer, journalist and pretty much the only employee at the *Junction Journal*, even though Mama had recently joined on as part of my research team, I had all the schedules for the holiday functions so I could take photos and report on them.

And because I was Holiday Junction's secret Merry Maker, it was nice to be able to have the inside scoop publicly, making the secret job much easier to perform.

The rules about the Merry Maker weren't clear. The only rules were these: no one could know, and a person-sized sign in the shape of the holiday had to be planted in the area where the Merry Maker wanted the holiday's last hurrah to take place. No one had ever known if co-Merry Makers existed, but I decided on that rule when Darren caused Mama to find out about my secret identity.

"Yes, they did." I stared into his dark eyes, resisting the urge to curl up on my tiptoes and kiss him. Instead, I reached up and mussed the longer curls in his dark hair.

"Stop." He batted me away. "Seriously. Do you like it?"

"I love it." I twisted my shoulders toward the amphitheater. A huge wooden cutout of a decorated Easter egg was placed near it. "It's a perfect place to end the festival. And the Mad Fiddlers are playing too."

I hadn't picked the amphitheater as the final hurrah for the festival because Darren's band was playing—not that I didn't choose that spot for that reason. Even though Darren and I had become co-Merry Makers, which I suspected was a first after hundreds of years, and I was wildly attracted to him, I wanted his band to be popular. If I had the power to let them be part of the final Easter celebration, I was going to do that.

"Thank you," he said, his eyes softening under his thick dark brows. "I know you suggested it for me."

He leaned in just enough to get my heart racing and my mind believing he was about to kiss me. Right there. In front of everyone.

A bloodcurdling scream made us jerk apart and look to see who was in desperate need of help.

The six Easter Bunnies scattered in different directions. Make that seven, because the one Mama was standing over lay flat on his fluffy back. Colorfully decorated Easter eggs had spilled out of the white basket and were strewn all around the costumed person auditioning for the part.

Mama brought her hands over her mouth and screamed, "The Easter Bunny is dead!"

Chocolate Bunny Betrayal is now available to purchase or in Kindle Unlimited.

If you enjoyed reading this book as much as I enjoyed writing it then be sure to return to the Amazon page and leave a review.

Go to Tonyakappes.com for a full reading order of my novels and while there join my newsletter. You can also find links to Facebook, Instagram and Goodreads.

Join like-minded readers like YOU in the Cozy Krew Facebook Group for dream casting, fan theories, and live Q & A's. It's like a BIG GIANT BOOK CLUB! But if you want to have your own book club, be sure you let me know! I love to send goodies.

Also By Tonya Kappes

A Camper and Criminals Cozy Mystery
BEACHES, BUNGALOWS, & BURGLARIES
DESERTS, DRIVERS, & DERELICTS
FORESTS, FISHING, & FORGERY
CHRISTMAS, CRIMINALS, & CAMPERS
MOTORHOMES, MAPS, & MURDER
CANYONS, CARAVANS, & CADAVERS
HITCHES, HIDEOUTS, & HOMICIDE
ASSAILANTS, ASPHALT, & ALIBIS
VALLEYS, VEHICLES & VICTIMS
SUNSETS, SABBATICAL, & SCANDAL
TENTS, TRAILS, & TURMOIL
KICKBACKS, KAYAKS, & KIDNAPPING
GEAR, GRILLS, & GUNS
EGGNOG, EXTORTION, & EVERGREENS
ROPES, RIDDLES, & ROBBERIES
PADDLERS, PROMISES, & POISON
INSECTS, IVY, & INVESTIGATIONS
OUTDOORS, OARS, & OATHS
WILDLIFE, WARRANTS, & WEAPONS
BLOSSOMS, BARBEQUE, & BLACKMAIL
LANTERNS, LAKES, & LARCENY
JACKETS, JACK-O-LANTERN, & JUSTICE
SANTA, SUNRISES, & SUSPICIONS
VISTAS, VICES, & VALENTINES
ADVENTURE, ABDUCTION, & ARREST
RANGERS, RV'S, & REVENGE
CAMPFIRES, COURAGE, & CONVICTS
TRAPPING, TURKEYS, & THANKSGIVING
GIFTS, GLAMPING, & GLOCKS
ZONING, ZEALOTS, & ZIPLINES

HAMMOCKS, HANDGUNS, & HEARSAY

Kenni Lowry Mystery Series
FIXIN' TO DIE
SOUTHERN FRIED
AX TO GRIND
SIX FEET UNDER
DEAD AS A DOORNAIL
TANGLED UP IN TINSEL
DIGGIN' UP DIRT
BLOWIN' UP A MURDER

Killer Coffee Mystery Series
SCENE OF THE GRIND
MOCHA AND MURDER
FRESHLY GROUND MURDER
COLD BLOODED BREW
DECAFFEINATED SCANDAL
A KILLER LATTE
HOLIDAY ROAST MORTEM
DEAD TO THE LAST DROP
A CHARMING BLEND NOVELLA (CROSSOVER WITH MAGICAL CURES MYSTERY)
FROTHY FOUL PLAY
SPOONFUL OF MURDER
BARISTA BUMP-OFF
CAPPUCCINO CRIMINAL

Holiday Cozy Mystery
FOUR LEAF FELONY
MOTHER'S DAY MURDER
A HALLOWEEN HOMICIDE
NEW YEAR NUISANCE
CHOCOLATE BUNNY BETRAYAL

APRIL FOOL'S ALIBI
FATHER'S DAY MURDER
THANKSGIVING TREACHERY
SANTA CLAUSE SURPRISE

Mail Carrier Cozy Mystery
STAMPED OUT
ADDRESS FOR MURDER
ALL SHE WROTE
RETURN TO SENDER
FIRST CLASS KILLER
POST MORTEM
DEADLY DELIVERY
RED LETTER SLAY

Magical Cures Mystery Series
A CHARMING CRIME
A CHARMING CURE
A CHARMING POTION (novella)
A CHARMING WISH
A CHARMING SPELL
A CHARMING MAGIC
A CHARMING SECRET
A CHARMING CHRISTMAS (novella)
A CHARMING FATALITY
A CHARMING DEATH (novella)
A CHARMING GHOST
A CHARMING HEX
A CHARMING VOODOO
A CHARMING CORPSE
A CHARMING MISFORTUNE
A CHARMING BLEND (CROSSOVER WITH A KILLER COFFEE
COZY)
A CHARMING DECEPTION

A Southern Magical Bakery Cozy Mystery Serial
A SOUTHERN MAGICAL BAKERY

A Ghostly Southern Mystery Series
A GHOSTLY UNDERTAKING
A GHOSTLY GRAVE
A GHOSTLY DEMISE
A GHOSTLY MURDER
A GHOSTLY REUNION
A GHOSTLY MORTALITY
A GHOSTLY SECRET
A GHOSTLY SUSPECT

A Southern Cake Baker Series
(WRITTEN UNDER MAYEE BELL)
CAKE AND PUNISHMENT
BATTER OFF DEAD

Spies and Spells Mystery Series
SPIES AND SPELLS
BETTING OFF DEAD
GET WITCH or DIE TRYING

A Laurel London Mystery Series
CHECKERED CRIME
CHECKERED PAST
CHECKERED THIEF

A Divorced Diva Beading Mystery Series
A BEAD OF DOUBT SHORT STORY
STRUNG OUT TO DIE
CRIMPED TO DEATH

Olivia Davis Paranormal Mystery Series

About Tonya

Tonya has written over 100 novels, all of which have graced numerous bestseller lists, including the USA Today. *Best known for stories charged with emotion and humor and filled with flawed characters, her novels have garnered reader praise and glowing critical reviews. She lives with her husband and a very spoiled rescue cat named Ro. Tonya grew up in the small southern Kentucky town of Nicholasville. Now that her four boys are grown men, Tonya writes full-time in her camper she calls her SHAMPER (she-camper).*

Learn more about her be sure to check out her website tonyakappes.com. Find her on Facebook, Twitter, BookBub, and Instagram

Sign up to receive her newsletter, where you'll get free books, exclusive bonus content, and news of her releases and sales.

If you liked this book, please take a few minutes to leave a review now! Authors (Tonya included) really appreciate this, and it helps draw more readers to books they might like. Thanks!

Cover artist: Mariah Sinclair: The Cover Vault

Made in the USA
Las Vegas, NV
19 May 2023